THE JOURNAL

The Journal

To Santiago,
Best wishes - Enjoy
the read!
Lois Donovan

Lois Donovan

RONSDALE PRESS

THE JOURNAL
Copyright © 2015 Lois Donovan

RONSDALE PRESS
3350 West 21st Avenue, Vancouver, B.C., Canada V6S 1G7
www.ronsdalepress.com

Typesetting: Julie Cochrane, in Minion 12 pt on 16
Cover Art & Design: Nancy de Brouwer, Massive Graphic Design
Paper: Ancient Forest Friendly "Silva" (FSC) — 100% post-consumer waste,
    totally chlorine-free and acid-free

Ronsdale Press wishes to thank the following for their support of its publishing program: the Canada Council for the Arts, the Government of Canada through the Canada Book Fund, the British Columbia Arts Council and the Province of British Columbia through the British Columbia Book Publishing Tax Credit program.

Library and Archives Canada Cataloguing in Publication

Donovan, Lois, 1955–, author
    The journal / Lois Donovan.

Issued in print and electronic formats.
ISBN 978-1-55380-350-8 (paper)
ISBN 978-1-55380-351-5 (ebook) / ISBN 978-1-55380-352-2 (pdf)

    I. Title.

PS8607.O68J69 2015   jC813'.6   C2014-907010-1   C2014-907012-8

At Ronsdale Press we are committed to protecting the environment. To this end we are working with Canopy (formerly Markets Initiative) and printers to phase out our use of paper produced from ancient forests. This book is one step towards that goal.

Printed in Canada by Marquis Printing, Quebec

To my parents,
Ron and Islay Capper,
for giving me roots and
wings — thank you

ACKNOWLEDGEMENTS

It takes a village to raise a child . . . and to write a book. Many friends, fellow authors and family members provided encouragement and support, not to mention patient listening during the many versions of this book. You know who you are. Thank you. I would like to single out, for special thanks, the following individuals: Ron and Veronica Hatch at Ronsdale Press for their wise guidance and gentle nudging to raise the bar; my eagle-eye-aunt, Anna Mae Siegel, for cheerfully reading and editing countless pages throughout the journey; and my niece, Cassidy Capper, for being my teen reader and advisor, and for living the challenge of Kami's final decision. I am also pleased to recognize the ones who provide me with daily inspiration: Jared and Katie Young, the best son/daughter-in-law team ever; daughter Grace and husband Patrick, who get to ride the roller coaster alongside me and still manage to remain my biggest fans. I couldn't do it without you.

"I am only one, but still I am one.
I cannot do everything, but still I can do something;
and because I cannot do everything,
I will not refuse to do something that I can do."

— HELEN KELLER

CHAPTER 1

The House

OCTOBER, 2004

"Kami, are you ready?" Mom called from the kitchen.

"Yeah, I'm packed," I answered. I'd never be ready to leave.

A crumpled photo, still stuck to my mirror, was the only thing left to pack. The movers would arrive in a couple of days for the rest of the stuff. I pulled the picture off and flattened it between my palms. There we were, the perfect family, posed in front of an ice-cream shop in Edmonton. Mom smiled like a dainty Japanese doll, while Dad towered over her, grinning like Goofy, in his ripped, cut-off jeans and T-shirt. I was in the middle holding my dad's hand.

Mom used to say I was the perfect blend of the two of

them. My dark almond eyes were hers, but my straight black hair had a coppery sheen that showed up in the sunlight. I got that from my dad. That and my long legs.

Almost three years ago, on my tenth birthday, Dad promised he would come for a visit and take me out to my favourite restaurant, but something came up and he bailed. That's when I squashed the picture into a ball and threw it in the trash. The next day I took it out and stuck it on my mirror. It was one of the few pictures I had of the three of us together.

"Kami!" Mom called again. "Baachan and Jiichan are here to take us to the airport." Baachan and Jiichan are what I call my Japanese grandparents.

I tucked the photo into the pocket of my carry-on bag and glanced at my cell phone. Two hours from now, Mom and I would be sitting on a plane, bound for Alberta, while my entire life stayed behind in Vancouver.

∽

My best friend, Becca, and her parents came to the airport to see us off. "I guess that's a *No* to the party room at the condo, huh?" Becca said, trying to be funny. We had been planning the best-ever birthday bash for our birthdays, which were only a week apart. My job had been to secure the party room at our condo.

"Do *not* cancel the party," I said. "I am totally flying back for my birthday. Maybe Vanessa could have it at her ginormous house. I bet she'd be all over that idea."

Becca's sad little smile said it all. She didn't believe I'd be back. But I was serious. My mother had screwed up everything else; I wasn't going to let her mess with my thirteenth birthday party.

As my mother and I pulled our carry-on bags down the corridor to security, I felt as though I was about to walk off a cliff, followed by a harsh landing.

My mother worked on her laptop for most of the flight while I read the newest Kenneth Oppel book, *Airborn*. After a huge hassle with picking up the rental car at the airport, we finally arrived at the hotel, where Mom buried herself in paperwork again, oblivious to the fact that she had just ripped my whole life apart. I sat in front of the TV, and ate chocolates from the gift basket that arrived just after we checked in. I wasn't in the mood to talk, anyway.

∽

We didn't go to see *the house* until the next morning. Mom thought it might be best to see it in daylight. It had been my grandparents' house and now it was ours. "We'll drive down Whyte Avenue to get a glimpse of the neighbourhood," Mom said, as we drove under a wrought-iron arch that said OLD STRATHCONA. "A lot has changed since the last time we were here," she commented. "Look at all the trendy little shops and eateries. And there's a Starbucks. You can't beat that for convenience." Mom couldn't start her day without her non-fat latte.

I stared out the window in silence. The stores weren't really my type of shopping, and everything else looked old. Really old. At least we were going to stay in the hotel until the movers came with our stuff. I was not looking forward to moving into my grandparents' old house.

Mom pulled off Whyte Avenue at 104th Street. We drove by a large brick building with the words PUBLIC LIBRARY stamped into the concrete moulding at the top. Then she turned down one of the side streets.

"This is it," she said, pulling the rental car into the long driveway of what was easily the largest house on the street. "Do you remember it?"

"It's bigger and older than I remembered."

"It's spacious," Mom agreed, parking the car in front of the fancy brick garage. Pointing to the garage, she said, "This old carriage house is something else, isn't it? Your Grandpa Anderson's pride and joy. He once told me that, back in the 1920s, the original owner converted an old carriage house into a garage with a turntable for motor cars. I don't remember the exact technology of how it worked, but it moved the car around so that the driver didn't have to back down the long driveway."

"Cool," I said, getting out of the car. I stared up at the massive brick house, shielding my eyes from the morning sun. Brown shingles popped up all over the roof, like a scared porcupine, and paint peeled in yellow curls from the window trim, making the place look kind of creepy. For a minute I even thought I saw a face looking out at me from one of the windows.

Mom pulled a set of keys from her purse. "Let's hope the inside is in better condition."

"Good luck with that," I muttered, following her up the cracked concrete stairs to the front door.

Mom turned the key in the lock and gave the door a solid shove.

"What if the inside *is* just as bad?" I said, peering past her into the dim entryway. "I mean, what if it's horrible and we don't want to live here?"

"That's a possibility," Mom said, feeling for the light switch.

I stepped into the foyer and looked around. To the left were large double doors that probably led to the living room. Mom disappeared down the long hallway, mumbling something about checking out the kitchen. I was more intrigued by the cool coat nook, tucked between the foyer and the narrow staircase that led to the second floor. I slipped off my runners and sat on the bench that outlined the u-shaped room. A sliver of a memory flitted through my brain. I was really little and hiding in the coats. Dad grabbed my legs, which were still dangling in full view. It's funny the things you remember.

On the outside wall, a stained-glass blue jay watched me from his stained-glass tree branch. "Do you remember the blue jay?" I asked Mom, who had reappeared from the kitchen.

"I do. The stained glass in this house was always my favourite part." She opened the double doors into the living room, then stopped. Glued to the spot.

"Oh my gosh," I said under my breath. The entire living room was full of my grandparents' stuff. I half-expected Grandma to appear any minute, offering milk and cookies. But Grandma died three years ago, when I had just started grade five. We didn't make it to the funeral. My grandfather moved soon after that to live with my Aunt Linda in PEI. I guess he didn't want to live in this big house all alone. Who could blame him?

"This is ridiculous," Mom fumed. "When the lawyer said that there may still be some things in the house, this was not what I expected."

"Maybe the movers can take some of this old stuff with them, when they drop ours off," I said. But the truth was, I couldn't picture any of our sleek leather or chrome-trimmed glass in this house. It was going to look totally weird.

"Hmm." Mom's forehead wrinkled under her smooth black hair. She took a small notebook out of her purse. "When your grandfather went to live with Aunt Linda, someone should have cleared out the house." I had a feeling the *someone* she referred to was my father, but I didn't say anything.

Everywhere it was the same. Furniture, paintings, knick-knacks. Mom groaned a lot, making notes on her trusty pad. I trailed along behind as we climbed the stairs to the second floor. What had she got us into?

"I suppose you want this big bedroom," I said, peering into the largest room on the floor. It was the only room that appeared to have escaped my grandmother's decorating. The walls were painted a dark taupe colour and the ornamental odds and ends were conspicuously absent.

"No. I don't want a bedroom up here, so you can have your pick."

"What do you mean? Are there more bedrooms somewhere?"

"The main floor has far more rooms than we need. I've already decided I'm going to make over one of those rooms — the formal dining room, perhaps. We won't need that and I don't want to be running up and down stairs all day." Mom checked her watch. "My meeting is in less than an hour so we'd better run. I have no idea what the traffic will be like."

"I can't picture us living here," I said. "We're not really the type."

"What type is that?"

"You know, the old-house-filled-with-old-furniture type."

"It's a historic house, Kami, and antique furniture is extremely valuable. Lots of people collect antique furniture."

"But not us," I pointed out.

"No, not us." Mom sighed and tucked her little book away in her purse. "We'll probably give most of it away to Goodwill. First on the list is a cleaning service." Mom turned abruptly and headed for the stairs.

"Maybe I could stay here and pick out my bedroom. I could start planning where my stuff will go," I suggested, taking the stairs two at a time. "It would give me something to do." Anything was better than sitting around at Mom's office with a bunch of strangers gawking at me and asking dumb questions.

"Don't be absurd, Kami. You can't stay here by yourself. No, you can bring your book with you to the office and read while I'm in my meeting, as we planned."

"I finished my book on the plane and your meetings go on forever."

"We should never have stopped here this morning. I have no time for all this fussing about."

"Are you going to hire before-and-after-school care for me, too?"

Mom frowned, as though she hadn't considered this fact.

"I'll be fine," I insisted. "I'm almost thirteen and you treat me as though I'm still in grade school."

"You'd prefer to stay in this dusty old house by yourself than in a clean, brightly lit office with a swivel chair?"

"A swivel chair, Mom? Seriously? I'm not five."

Mom huffed impatiently. "I suppose you'd be okay for a couple of hours."

"Of course I will. Anyway, I'm not in the mood to meet a bunch of people." I could tell she was thinking it over.

"Fine, but don't go wandering off somewhere and get yourself lost. You can go to Whyte Avenue and get a snack, but that's it. Don't talk to anyone, and come straight back."

"Thanks, Mom, and don't worry. It's pretty hard to get lost between here and Whyte Ave."

She took the house key off her set of keys. "Don't forget to lock the door if you go out and don't lose the key. I haven't had a chance to make a copy yet." Mom's forehead creased as though she were trying to remember more rules.

"I have my cell phone. I'll be fine. I won't even jump on a city bus and go exploring."

"Small wonder I'm getting grey hair." Mom opened the little side zipper on her purse and produced a twenty-dollar bill. "In case you're hungry."

I stuffed the twenty into the pocket of my jeans. "Thanks. Now just go already, before you're late for your meeting."

I waved as Mom cautiously backed down the driveway, and kept watching until she disappeared down the street. Then I sat on the dusty old sofa and took a deep breath. Reality stared me in the face from every corner. We were actually in Edmonton. Our condo in Vancouver was up for sale. In a few days I would be going to a new school where I didn't know anyone. And I would be seeing my father, whom I hadn't heard from in two years. I squeezed my eyes shut, not wanting to think about any of it. It was all because of that dumb letter.

CHAPTER 2

The Letter

THE LETTER ARRIVED on Monday, the second week of school. I had just found out I was one of two eighth-graders who had made the senior soccer team. I could hardly wait to phone Mom at her office and tell her the news.

When I opened the door to the condo, Mom was sitting at the kitchen table, a letter dangling from her fingers. "What's up? I didn't expect you to be home yet." I figured it had to be something really good, or something really bad. And from the look on her face, I was pretty sure it wasn't good.

"Sit down, Kami. We need to talk."

I dropped my backpack on the kitchen chair, not sure I

wanted to hear the news. "Let me get a snack first, I'm starving."

"This letter arrived at my office today," Mom said.

I grabbed a muffin from the tin and poured myself a glass of milk.

"It's from your Grandfather Anderson's lawyer."

"Is that bad? Did something happen to Grandpa?"

"No, nothing has happened," Mom said. "But your grandfather does have an outrageous request that he insists I talk to you about." She shook her head, muttering under her breath. "I didn't expect something like this."

"We haven't heard from him in ages. What's going on?"

"I'll read you the letter."

It was a little tricky to sort out all the lawyer lingo, and I wasn't sure I understood it. "So, Grandpa wants to give me a house?" I asked. "I don't get it."

"That makes two of us." Mom shook her head again. "I can't imagine what has got into your grandfather."

"So, I *am* getting a house?"

"It's not that straightforward, Kami. There are conditions. Listen to the rest of the letter."

"*Kami Ellen Anderson is required to reside at the aforementioned property, with her mother, until the time of her eighteenth birthday on October 27, 2009, at which time all conditions will be removed and ownership will be transferred . . .*"

"We have to live at the house?" I interrupted. "Grandpa knows we don't live in Edmonton."

"We aren't going to live in your grandparents' old house.

This is insane." Mom put the letter back in the envelope as though that settled the matter.

Mom was right. It was crazy. But it bugged me that she didn't at least ask my opinion. "Are we going to talk about it?"

"There's nothing to talk about. I told you it was outrageous."

"What if *I* want to move to Edmonton?" I asked, making a point.

"Oh, Kami. You're always wishing for spilled milk to return to the glass."

That was Mom for you. Some weird saying, instead of actually answering the question. "I don't even know why you told me about the letter." I grabbed my backpack and went to my room. No point in telling her about the soccer team now.

I tried to do my homework, but all I could think about was the strange letter. Why was my grandfather offering *me* his house? This had to be my father's idea. Not that it mattered. Mom would never move to Edmonton. I would have bet a year's worth of allowance on it. I was *that* sure.

The next few days Mom spent long hours at work, but I was too busy to mind. The teachers piled on the homework, soccer practice was almost every day after school, and Becca called constantly with questions about the joint birthday party we were planning.

The lawyer's letter wasn't really on the radar now. I figured if my grandfather wanted me to have the house, I'd get it when I was old enough to actually own a house, and we'd deal with it then.

But on Friday, when Mom came home from work, I knew something was up. I tried to talk to her about the birthday party, but she gave one-word answers and didn't really listen. It was super annoying. "So, you'll do it?" I said, finally. "You'll book the party room for October 23rd, so Becca and I can go ahead with our plans?"

"A party? Oh, Kami, there's no rush. A lot could happen between now and then."

"Yeah, like a lot of other people booking the room," I muttered.

"Something interesting came up at work today," Mom said, changing the subject.

Work. I should have known.

"The City of Edmonton is embarking on a substantial inner-city renewal project and they need an urban designer to head up the team." Mom set out the sushi she had picked up at the market, while I got out the dishes.

"Edmonton? How weird is that?"

There was a long pause, then Mom continued. "The City Manager responsible for the project wondered if I'd be interested in taking it on."

"What?" I almost dropped the plates I was carrying. "You aren't seriously considering the job. We're not moving. You said so yourself."

"For years you've complained about not seeing your father often enough. This is your opportunity."

I stared at my mother — stunned. "What happened to *outrageous*? *Insane*?"

"Calm down, Kami. It wouldn't be a permanent move. Just for a few years, until you own the house. By then, the project would be finished, you could sell the house, and we could move back to Vancouver."

"You're crazy," I practically shouted the words. "In a few years, I'll be too old for the senior soccer team, and my friends will be gone to university. I'm not moving to Edmonton just because you got a job offer."

"It's not a *job offer*, it's a career opportunity, in the same way that your owning a house is an opportunity. How many eighteen-year-olds do you know who own property? I've done some research. That place in Old Strathcona will be worth a small fortune."

"Why did the City of Edmonton contact you about this job anyway?" Nothing happened in my mother's world by accident.

Mom began washing a pile of green stuff for the salad. "I thought you'd be excited."

"I've asked Dad to come out to see me and he hasn't called or sent a card for two years. I wanted you to take me to Edmonton during the summer holidays, but you didn't have time. Now you expect me to do the happy dance because it suits your plans to move to Edmonton. News flash! I have a life too. And I don't want to drop everything for Dad, or you, or some old house."

"I'm sorry you feel that way, Kami," Mom said, in the same tone you would say you wished it wasn't raining out.

"What about Baachan and Jiichan?" I continued.

"We'll visit. Your grandparents are still young. We'll move back in time to support them in their old age. It will all work out."

Reality hit me like a fork of lightning. "Oh my gosh. You've already taken the job, haven't you?"

A long, exhausted sigh was the only answer.

I ran off to my room and pulled the door closed — hard. I wasn't the least bit hungry.

∾

So, here I was, in Old Strathcona, my new neighbourhood. Five years, Mom had said. It might as well be a life sentence.

I wrote my name in the dust on the coffee table. What *was* I going to do all day?

Bong! The sound startled me half out of my skin. Grandma and Grandpa's old chime clock. I ventured into the front hall. There was the culprit. The old clock had bonged the half-hour. I stopped to look at the black-and-white photos that hung beside the clock. One was of a sombre-looking couple with a little girl dressed in a frilly outfit and wearing a crazy-looking hat. Another showed two pilots in an open cockpit plane with the title MERCY FLIGHT written on it, whatever that was. Wow. These photos were really old. I wondered if I was related to any of these people.

Full of strange noises and old furniture, this old house was feeling a little creepy, and I began to think my stubbornness about hanging out in Mom's office had backfired. A bookstore or library would kill some time — which reminded me that we had passed a library on the drive here. If I remembered correctly, it was only a couple of blocks away. Perfect.

I dashed upstairs to the bathroom for a pit stop before heading out. The bathroom was really large with an old-fashioned tub sitting under a yellow and blue flowery stained-glass window. It was kind of cool, but I would miss my ensuite. The condo might have been small but it had two master bedrooms, which meant that I had my own bathroom and a walk-in closet. This house was full of bedrooms, but they had the tiniest closets I'd ever seen — and no bathrooms.

When I came out, I noticed another set of stairs at the very end of the hall. These steps were painted brown, but most of the paint had worn off. Memories of a blanket-draped table and plates of animal crackers began to emerge as I climbed the creaky steps. Grandma had used the attic as a sewing room. She used to let me build forts there sometimes while she worked.

The door at the top of the stairs was closed. I twisted the knob and slowly pushed, half expecting something to jump out at me. Nothing jumped and nothing sinister appeared. Just a bunch of boxes. Even my over-active imagination couldn't conjure up something evil about a stuffy old storage room.

Squeezing between the boxes I managed to get to the large dormer window, which overlooked the street. I cranked the window open, enjoying the gust of crisp air that blew in. Much better.

There was something warm and cozy about attic rooms with their sloped walls that curled into the ceiling. Grandma's sewing machine used to be in the corner beside the window. She would sit there, humming alongside the machine as she sewed shapes onto coloured squares for her newest quilt. All the grandchildren got one. Mine had little white ducks sewn onto light-green squares, but it had disappeared a long time ago.

The boxes faded away as I stretched back to those faint memories. Dad would hang blankets over Grandma's cutting table, making a perfect fort. I'd bring up all my stuffies, and Grandpa would set up an electric camping lantern. Such a happy place. And just like that, my decision was made. This would be my room. Up here, I could create a comfy loft and forget that there was a whole rambling house below. This would be my special fort.

CHAPTER 3

The Journal

THE LIBRARY COULD WAIT. I needed to clear out the boxes before Mom got back. She would hate all the fussing around and would want me to pick one of the five bedrooms on the second floor. At least storage space shouldn't be a problem. I zipped down the back stairs to find the best spot.

The three rooms overlooking the yard were automatically ruled out. There was no point in giving the boxes a room with a view. The large bedroom that Mom didn't want would make a good space for electronics where I could hang out with friends — the friends I hoped were out there, some-where. That left the room at the top of the stairs. Small. Not much furniture. Perfect.

Carrying the boxes down the stairs and along the hall was not much fun, but I didn't mind. My own special loft. I could hardly wait. Some of the boxes were not too difficult to manage. Others felt like a load of bricks. Those ones I pushed against the end wall of the attic. Good enough. Knowing my mother, most of them were headed to the same fate — in a round bin.

By the time I was down to the final box, the little room was pretty crowded. This last one could just go on top of the little bed for now. I didn't see the loose throw rug. My right foot caught the edge of it, and the next thing I knew, the box and I were airborne. My elbow bashed into the end of the bed just before my butt hit the floor. "Owwww!" I yelled at the offending rug. I looked sideways at the upside-down box and groaned. There had been a definite crack when the box landed and even though my elbow and butt were extremely sore, I didn't think any part of me had cracked. Well, I thought, getting up slowly, it was probably junk anyway. Or a family heirloom belonging to my grandfather. That wouldn't be good.

I peeled off the layers of packing tape and opened the box. A small black and gold desk globe looked as if it had broken off its metal base. Yikes. I gently took out both pieces and set them on the bureau. At least the pieces weren't broken. That was something. Underneath was a framed photo, the glass broken in half. Glass could be replaced. The photo itself didn't look damaged. Whew!

Being careful not to cut myself on the broken glass, I

picked up the picture for a closer look. Black lettering across the top announced, 75TH ANNIVERSARY FLIGHT, JANUARY 2, 2004. In the photo, two men stood on a snowy runway in front of a small plane. The caption at the bottom read: *The Wop May-Vic Horner Mercy Flight, Edmonton to Fort Vermillion, January 2, 1929. Re-enacted by sons, Denny May and Bob Horner.*

Mercy flight? Wasn't that what was written on that black-and-white photo in the front hall? I raced downstairs to check it out. There it was — a close-up of the pilots in an open cockpit, with MERCY FLIGHT printed boldly across the top. On the wing of the plane were two autographs I hadn't noticed before. The top one read *Vic Horner* and the bottom one looked like *Wop May*. This must be a photo of the original flight in 1929. Grandma and Grandpa must have known the pilots. I ran back upstairs and looked again at the coloured picture of the re-enactment flight. Seventy-five years had made a huge difference in aircraft technology. The pilot's sons, Denny and Bob, were standing in front of a sleek prop plane with five windows. I still didn't know what the Mercy Flight was, but it was obvious that the re-enactment flight had been a lot more comfortable. Just then, I noticed the tiny gold lettering in the corner. *Michael Anderson Photography.*

A tingle of excitement raced through my veins. My father had been the photographer? Did that mean this box of stuff was his? Suddenly, I had a keen interest in discovering what else was in the box. I set the picture beside the globe and con-

tinued taking things out of the box. There was a stack of old
'80s cds and an ugly greenish-brown ceramic coffee mug that
remained intact — of course. A nice one would have broken.
Murphy's Law. Under that appeared to be mostly calendars
with photos of scenery and wildlife. My shoulders sagged. I
didn't know exactly what I was looking for, but a bunch of
old calendars wasn't it.

I was about to put everything back in, when I spotted the
worn leather cover of a little book buried at the very bottom.
A tattered piece of lace wrapped around it, binding it closed.
Maybe this was my dad's too, from when he was a kid or
something. It looked really old. My fingers, jittery with anticipation, unwound the ratty tie, then opened the cover. The
name, *Helen Mitchell*, was written in loopy black script. Who
the heck was Helen Mitchell? Then I saw the date. Oh my
gosh. 1929? Really? Leaving the open box on the floor, I
climbed onto the lumpy bed and began to read.

JANUARY 1, 1929

*This journal was my special Christmas gift from Mom and
Dad, but I waited for the new year to begin writing in it. I love
the creamy white pages and the soft leather cover. It must have
been very expensive. I will use my finest hand to write on the
faint blue lines. Perhaps I'll paste in newspaper articles written
by my father (and sometimes my mother, but no one is supposed to know that). Someday I might be a stringer, too. Mom
says by the time I grow up, women will be able to write real*

articles with their own by-line and not be stuck writing the So-
ciety Page nonsense. The by-line is the part that says, by . . . and
then your name. My dad taught me that. This year will be fab-
ulous because I will turn thirteen. (Just like me. How weird is
that?)

Thirteen sounds so grown up. Mother says I can get my hair
bobbed like Cousin Elizabeth. She is fifteen years old and very
fashionable. I can hardly wait.

Last night mother and father let me stay up until midnight
at their annual New Year's Eve party. My friend Hattie was so
jealous. Her parents never let her stay up to see the new year in.
Daddy wrote a New Year's Eve article and I hope he mentioned
our party. The article will be printed in tomorrow's paper, be-
cause there is no paper today.

I turned to the next page. The promised article — yellowed
with age — was still legible.

WHISTLES SHRIEK AND BELLS CLANG AS EDMONTON GREETS ARRIVAL OF THE NEW YEAR

Snow spread its soft white mantle over the ground and
frost put a tang in the air, to give just the proper touch
to Edmonton's greeting of a brand new year. With
shrieking of whistles and clanging of bells with hilari-
ous gatherings everywhere, the city bade goodbye to
1928 and welcomed with high hopes another twelve-
month period. Festivities of every description marked
the birth of the new year . . .

The words blurred together and coloured specks smeared my vision. Before I knew what was happening, the entire room spun into a kaleidoscope of whirling colour. Rubbing my eyes did nothing to clear the crazy colours, and now every blood vessel in my head pulsed with the flashing spots. I lay back on the bed and tried to relax. Vision disturbances often appeared right before a migraine episode, but it had never been anything like this. The pounding increased. I held my head tightly, hoping to prevent my skull from exploding, and slowly sat up. The moment my feet touched the floor, two things happened: first, the pounding drumbeat in my head subsided, and second, I opened my eyes. What I saw scared me more than the flashing colours.

CHAPTER 4

The Party

THE BOXES WERE GONE. The bed had a colourful quilt on it, and there was a long narrow dresser with a fancy silver brush and comb set on the top. Was this another memory? A vision of what the room looked like when I was little? I scrunched the quilt between my fingers. You couldn't feel a memory with your fingers, could you? As I contemplated this idea, I became aware of voices somewhere outside the door. I strained my ears. The voices were coming from inside the house. Not good. A stinky, smoky smell was drifting into the room as well. None of this helped calm the panic that clenched my stomach.

I opened the bedroom door. The voices grew louder and the smell of smoke stronger. Not knowing what else to do, I ventured slowly down the dark stairs.

"Lordy, Jack, don't you teach the poor girl to dance," a woman said, her laugh tinkling like crystal. I crouched on the stairs, inside the shadows, afraid to move. Jazzy music and the din of chatter filled the air. What was happening? Becca and I had read *Ghosts of Vancouver* at a sleepover once. In some of the stories ghost people appeared and moved things around or played pranks on the real people, but I couldn't recall any of them actually speaking. These voices seemed very loud for ghost people.

I crept down a little further and peeked through the banister. A sparkling chandelier lit the elegant foyer, and beyond that the living room buzzed with men and women, dressed in all the finery of an old-time Hollywood movie. Men in tails smoked, oblivious to the blue fog that enveloped them, while the women gathered at the couches in their shiny satin gowns, watching the dance floor. These people did not look like the disgruntled spirits that Becca and I had read about.

A woman in a red silky dress, covered in fringes commanded everyone's attention on the dance floor. Beside her, wiggling and waggling to the jazzy music, a young girl imitated the flamboyant dancer. A man, maybe the girl's father, made fun of the dancers, showing off his own outrageous moves to the enjoyment of the guests. The young girl looked my way, but didn't appear to see me.

Fur coats and fur-trimmed boots filled the little coat room and the glass blue jay on the branch sat in darkness. It was cold and dark. Winter. The realization slowly seeped into my brain. This was Helen's house and tonight was New Year's Eve.

The phone in the hallway jangled, startling me and I scooted further up the stairs out of view.

"You want to speak to Captain May?" the man, who I figured must be Helen's father, shouted into the mouthpiece. "Urgent you say? Hold on. I'll get him for you."

Sitting in the shadows, I contemplated my predicament. I didn't want to go back upstairs, but I obviously couldn't go downstairs either. The music stopped at that moment and the host announced that it was time to prepare for the countdown. In the calm of the announcement, I heard the voice of the man who was wanted on the phone. "Diphtheria? That's terrible. Yes. I understand. I'll do my best. I'll have to find out if there is a plane available." There was a click as he replaced the receiver.

"You're not leaving already, Wop, my friend?" A man's voice boomed over the music that had started up again. "We're preparing for the countdown." I held my breath, afraid of being discovered.

Wop? Wasn't that one of the names on the old photograph in the front hallway? Oh my gosh. He was one of the pilots. It was such an odd name. It had to be the same guy.

"There's diphtheria up north at the Little Red River Settlement," the one named Wop, was saying. "Dr. Hammond sent a telegram wanting me to fly some antidote serum up there, but I don't even know if any aeroplanes are available."

"The weather is bitter. You can't fly up there in a blizzard. What is he thinking?" the other man responded.

"He's thinking a lot of people are going to die if we don't get something up there fast."

"You killing yourself in a snowstorm is not going to save them. There's got to be a better way."

"If any planes are available, I'll go. I better tell Vi."

"You're a good man, Wop. Let me know if there's something I can do to help."

The two men had barely finished speaking when cheers of "Happy New Year!" erupted from the living room, accompanied by banging pots, whistles squealing, and horns honking. This was my chance to sneak back upstairs before everyone came looking for their coats.

The pounding in my head returned. I grabbed the railing with one hand and my head with the other as my vision blurred. The stairs beneath me tilted and spun like a carnival ride picking up speed. As the music faded away, the swaying slowed. I moved one foot ahead of the other up the stairs. When my vision cleared I could see the faded roses of the worn carpet beneath my feet once more. The voices were gone now, and no hint of smoke lingered in the air. I turned and crept back down the stairs, needing to see for myself. From the bottom landing, I peered into the silence of my grandparents' living room.

Tiredness pulled at my body, even as my mind raced. How it happened, I had no idea. But there had been a New Year's Eve party here. I was sure of it.

At the top of the stairs, I passed the open door of the storage room. Boxes were stacked against the wall. No bureau with a silver-handled brush and comb set was evident. I continued along to the back stairwell.

It was as though something had flung me into Helen's world, like Dorothy being blown into the Land of Oz. My legs wobbled as I climbed the squeaky steps to the attic. I grabbed my backpack from the floor by the window. Suddenly the library seemed like a great idea. I really didn't want to spend more time in the house alone. Before I even got my hoodie on, the phone in my pocket buzzed, startling me.

"Hello," I said, my voice as shaky as my knees.

"Hello Kami. How are you doing? Are you bored out of your mind?" my mother asked.

"No, not really." Breathe. Just breathe.

"You sound funny. Are you nervous? Maybe I shouldn't have left you alone in such a big, old house."

"No, it's fine. I'm fine."

"This meeting is dragging out longer than I expected, and then I have to meet with the architect as well. I'll be there two-ish, if you can manage until then." She paused. "Are you okay?"

No, I'm not okay, I'm flipping out of my sick and disturbed mind, I wanted to shout. "I was thinking of spending some time at the library," I said, trying to sound casual. "Could you pick me up there?"

"Actually, I need to get some measurements from the house before we go to the hotel so I'll call when I'm on my way. That will give you time to get back from the library. It's only a couple of blocks away — right?"

"Yeah, right. Okay, well, I'll see you later, then." I clicked off my phone and stuffed it into my hoodie pocket. Yeah, I'd be waiting out front. I was not coming back in this house today.

On my way downstairs, I stopped and looked in the storage room again. The journal was lying on the bed where I had left it. Was it possible to go back in time? It didn't seem possible. I picked up the journal and put it in my backpack. Leaving it lying around for my mother to find didn't seem like a good idea.

CHAPTER 5

Knights of the Air

THE BRISK AIR SMELLED of damp leaves and overripe apples. I breathed deeply, not minding a bit when the chilly breeze blew down the neck of my hoodie. This outing was just what I needed. I reached into my pocket, checking for the twenty-dollar bill. Good.

At the corner of Whyte Avenue and 105th Street, I spotted the familiar Starbuck's sign at the end of the block. Already I could taste the bittersweet chocolate with cool mounds of whipped cream melting into it.

I glanced into the store windows along the way. A consignment boutique featuring retro clothing. A health store of sorts displaying tarot cards and healing geodes. An antique furniture store. This neighbourhood had a unique personality. No question.

The line-up at Starbucks wasn't bad. I ordered my drink and a wrap, then snagged a window seat. I liked to watch people scurrying by on the sidewalk. But today I seemed to be studying every man in sight, in case he was my father. It was a ridiculous thing to do, but I couldn't help myself. I slurped the whip cream off my hot chocolate. After reading that crazy journal, I was more anxious than ever to connect with my father.

I pulled out my phone and checked the time. One o'clock. Mom would be back in about an hour. That gave me time to get to the library and load up on some books. I tossed my cup in the trash. On the way to the door, I spied some tasty-looking energy bars. With Mom's track record, her meeting could go on all afternoon. I bought two of the fruit-and-nut bars, then stuffed them into the pocket of my hoodie.

It wasn't hard to find the library. It was only a block off Whyte Avenue on 104th Street. Wide concrete stairs led to the tall double doors of the impressive brick building. According to the plaque, the building was erected in 1913. Helen's library. Goose bumps shivered up the back of my neck as I pulled open the heavy door.

Old card-catalogue drawers and photographs of the library's early days were on display just inside the door. Dark wood shelving lined the walls and cozy gas fireplaces warmed up matching reading areas on either side of the checkout desk. Other than the ugly grey security gates and the computers, you could tell they tried to keep the original look of the place. I set my backpack on one of the comfy chairs. A perfect spot to read and wait for Mom to finish up.

No one was at the library desk, but a sign advertising free internet was prominently displayed. All you needed was a current library card. Awesome. Mom never let me use the internet. She was like the computer police or something. I had to share her laptop and could only use it at the kitchen table and usually only for homework. Any time I tried to send an email, my mother hovered around, pretending she was cleaning up the kitchen. If I could use the internet at the library, I could send messages to Becca without having to worry about my mother snooping over my shoulder. That would be amazing. I could hardly wait to sign up.

Where was the librarian, anyway? I sat down on the chair, then reached into my backpack to get out a tissue. My fingers found the soft leather cover of Helen's diary. I pulled out the little pack of tissues, ignoring the book. Maybe I should choose some novels to sign out, while I waited for the clerk to come. But I didn't move. Instead, I reached back into my bag and pulled out the leather notebook. What if I read it here? The New Year's Eve party couldn't be here, in the library. That old house with its dusty memories must have sparked my over-active imagination. I'd read one entry to get over this mysterious journal mindset, then I'd look for some books to sign out.

I flipped past the first entry to a faded newspaper clipping of two pilots standing in front of a biplane. A fellow in a long overcoat appeared to be handing them a blanket-wrapped bundle. I checked the date at the top of the clipping. January 2, 1929. Shivers crept up my neck. I had a feeling I knew what this story was going to be about. I also knew I should close the book right then, and zip it into my backpack. That would be the smart thing. I began to read.

KNIGHTS OF THE AIR

Captain "Wop" May, with local bush pilot Victor Horner, is away into the cold blue of the northern skies on an errand of mercy. The airmen are carrying anti-toxin to Fort Vermillion to fight an outbreak of diphtheria that has already claimed victims. Captain Wop May had many a thrilling fight over the German lines in France. He was involved in the air battle with the famous Richthofen, that resulted in the death of that deadly German ace. He is today an even greater knight of the air than in 1918. Facing innumerable risks, he and his companion are away to save lives.

I tried to read more but my eyes refused to focus. The room tilted first one direction then another until dizziness forced me to close my eyes altogether. A chill shivered along my arms as my brain conjured up the cold of the swirling snow in the photo, and an intense pressure squeezed my skull making me feel nauseous. Gradually the dizziness subsided and I opened my eyes.

The library clerk at the checkout was staring at me, a strange look on her face, as if by simply sitting here, I had done something wrong. My legs wobbled as I walked toward the checkout desk. That's when I noticed a beautiful bronze statue of a young girl. I hadn't seen that when I walked in. A little girl, hands clasped, looked skyward. PRAYER OF FAITH, the card beside it read. It could have been me, when I was seven, begging God to make my father come back.

I was about to apply for a library card, when I realized that the statue wasn't the only thing that looked different. The checkout area didn't look the same, either. The security gates were missing. That's what it was. I turned toward the back wall where the computers had been, but they, too, were gone. My whole body began to shake.

I went back to where I was sitting, but my backpack was nowhere in sight. This was not good. I hurried down the few stairs to the door. Even before I opened it, I saw the snow. *No way*. When I stepped outside, an icy gust of wind blew snow into my face. Snow — like the middle of winter — not like the middle of October. I darted across the road. Tires screeched. A man in a black roadster yelled out the window, shaking an angry finger at me.

No computers. No backpack. Snow. An antique car. My brain tallied the information but refused to process it. I continued along 84th Avenue, anxious to find my grandparents' house. I could see it in the middle of the block when my runners slipped on a patch of ice and I went flying, landing hard on my elbow. I got to my feet, keeping the house in sight. I wasn't going to stop until I got to the attic, as though by merely reaching it, everything would return to normal.

I sprinted up the walkway to the front door, not even pausing to think about why the front door looked freshly painted or why it was unlocked. Halfway up the stairs, a girl appeared on her way down. She shrieked as if she had seen a monster. I froze on the spot.

"Mom!" the girl yelled. "There's a Chinese in our house."

The girl looked terrified as she backed up the stairs and disappeared.

"Helen, what on earth are you yelling about?" A woman in a print dress emerged from the kitchen. Then she spotted me, frozen to the stair, wondering what to do. "What in tarnation? Who in the name of all the saints are you?"

"I, I . . ." my voice faltered. "This is Helen's house?" was all I could think of to say.

"Helen," the woman shouted again. "Get down here this minute."

Helen reappeared at the top of the stairs.

"This girl seems to know you," the woman said crisply.

"She's lying. I've never met the likes of her before."

The woman raised her eyebrows, expecting an explanation.

"I thought this was my house," I explained. "So when you called for Helen, I was a little confused."

"There are no other houses in the neighbourhood that resemble this one."

"My mother and I just moved here and I got confused."

"Indeed." Helen's mother shot me a disapproving look.

Just then, Helen's father walked through the door. "Who do we have here?" he asked, looking surprised.

"This Chinese girl walked right into our house, just like that," Helen exclaimed. "She was on her way up the stairs when I caught her red-handed."

"For the record, I'm not Chinese," I said.

"Are too, I can tell by your slanty eyes." Helen jumped in before I could continue.

"They're almond shaped," I corrected, finding her to be very rude, "like my mother's eyes, and she is Japanese."

"Japanese, Chinese, what's the difference?" she answered.

"The important thing about her parents," Helen's father began impatiently, "is where they are right now. We have to get a move on. This flight is a big story for the paper, and we're short-staffed so I'm covering the story myself. We are darn well not going to be late."

"The girl seems to be lost, and I haven't the slightest idea who she is or where she came from," Helen's mother said.

"What's your name?" Mr. Mitchell asked.

"Kami Anderson," I answered. "I was sure the house I left this afternoon was this one, but obviously I was wrong."

"*Kami.*" The woman tried out the name as though she were sampling a new food. "What an unusual name. I don't think I've seen any of your people in this neighbourhood." Her eyebrows scrunched together.

"*My* people?" The heat prickled my cheeks.

"I'm not trying to upset you. I only mean that our neighbours are all British. There aren't any Chinese families in Strathcona." Mrs. Mitchell gave her husband a meaningful glance. "Or Japanese families," she added.

"C'mon Millie. I don't have all day. The girl can come with us, and we'll find her family when we get back." He turned to his daughter. "You two scallywags get your coats on, Lizzie is ready to roll."

"Jack, do you think that's wise? I mean, we have no idea who this girl is."

"If you want to stay with the girl, Millie, and get things sorted out, I understand. I do. But I've gotta go."

Mrs. Mitchell flattened her lips into a straight line. "I'm not staying with the girl."

"Already ladies. Lizzie and I will be waiting." Mr. Mitchell pulled up the collar of his coat and headed out the door.

Mrs. Mitchell muttered something under her breath as she grabbed a navy coat from the hooks in the coatroom, then picked out some red mittens and a scarf from a drawer under the bench seat. "Here, put these on," she said to me. That's when she noticed my striped runners. "What in heaven's name have you got on your feet?" she asked, not waiting for an answer. "Helen, run up to the attic and get those galoshes that your Aunt Kate brought over for you." Helen groaned as she stomped up the stairs.

It wasn't easy, but I squashed my runners into the ugly brown boots, and followed the Mitchells out to the car named Lizzie.

CHAPTER 6

Blatchford Field

ROUND BUG-EYE HEADLIGHTS glowed through the grey blanket of falling snow as Lizzie shuddered and shook on the skinniest tires I had ever seen. Worse than the über-narrow tires, however, was the conspicuous lack of glass in the vehicle's windows.

"It'll be a cold ride today," Helen's father called from the driver's seat. He pulled down the earflaps on his fur cap.

No kidding. I climbed into the back seat beside Helen, thinking this was a really bad idea. Helen tied down leather flaps that covered the window openings, but I couldn't see that making much of a difference. Meanwhile, I searched for a seat belt that didn't exist. Great.

A *cold ride*, was the understatement of the year. Even bundled in a blanket, with a scarf wrapped around my face, my teeth chattered worse than a nervous squirrel. We might as well be on a dogsled for all the protection Lizzie provided.

"You won't be disappointed you came," Helen's father yelled to me over the noise of the car and the wind. "These are world-class heroes you're seeing in action today."

"I told Hattie about seeing the pilots off," Helen said. "She couldn't believe I was getting to see a real aeroplane up close. Do you think Captain May will let me sit in it?" she asked her father.

"Sometime perhaps, but not today," he answered. "This is a mighty dangerous mission these fellows are embarking on, and you can't be pestering them."

Bouncing through the ruts of the snowy trail, I thought it would be a miracle if we arrived at our destination at all. So, when Mr. Mitchell pulled to a stop behind three other boxy vehicles, I felt a great sense of relief.

"Let's go, ladies." Mr. Mitchell scooted around to open his wife's door. Then he opened the trunk and got out a large tripod. "Here you go, girls." He handed Helen one end of the equipment, and I took the other end. Talk about heavy-duty. That thing weighed a ton.

"History is happening and yours truly is going to be the one to tell the story," Mr. Mitchell said, as though he were the one setting off on a major expedition.

We all trudged into the lone building that appeared to be dropped in the middle of the snowy field. Glad for the warmth of a closed building with no open windows, I took off the mittens Mrs. Mitchell had found for me, and rubbed my hands together.

"Come on. Let's go out and see the aeroplane," Helen said the minute we set down her father's gear. "There's nothing happening in here."

"Except warmth," I commented, but Helen was already halfway to the door.

"Just mind you don't make a nuisance of yourself," Mrs. Mitchell called after us. "I'll be out there shortly." She was chatting with a couple of women who I assumed were the pilots' wives. They appeared to be the only women around.

Out in the field, a small group gathered around the little biplane, which looked like a carnival ride — or a museum display — but not a mode of transportation.

"Gee, this is so exciting," Helen said, wasting no time in finding a spot close to the cockpit.

I recognized Captain May from the photo. His face was more serious than ever. Given the machine he had to depend on, he must be wondering if he and his buddy would survive the trip. I know that's what I'd be wondering.

By now everyone from the tiny airport was outside to see the pilots off, including Mrs. Mitchell, who was trying to scribble notes on a pad of paper while wearing wool gloves. Helen and I huddled with the others, watching the final preparations. The pilots appeared to be checking and re-checking everything as they readied the plane for flight.

Finally, a man carrying a blanket-wrapped bundle walked over to the pilots. They all posed for Mr. Mitchell to take a picture, and an eerie chill settled over me that had nothing to do with the weather. I was witnessing the photograph from the journal. First, the New Year's Eve party and now the Mission of Mercy flight. Somehow, I had discovered a portal between the two time periods, and it seemed to be connected to that journal.

"How will you keep the serum from freezing?" Mrs. Mitchell asked the pilots, bringing me back to what was happening.

"We've installed charcoal burners in the rear of the cockpit behind the back seat," one of the pilots replied.

"We're hoping it will keep our feet from freezing as well," his buddy chimed in.

The medicine safely stowed, the pilots pulled heavy overcoats over their layers of winter clothing and donned their hats and goggles. A woman waved to the men as they climbed into their seats.

"That's Mrs. May," Helen said.

Suddenly, I remembered the two energy bars that I had in my hoodie. These pilots had hours ahead of them, and they wouldn't be stopping at Tim Hortons along the way. I fumbled under the coat to see if they were still there. Yes, they were. Excellent. I raced up to the cockpit and handed Captain May the two bars.

"For energy," I said, shouting over the wind. Captain May nodded and smiled as he put one in his coat and handed the other to his partner. "You're going to make it," I added. "Seventy-five years from now, the flight will be re-enacted in your honour." I wasn't sure if he heard me, but I hoped he did. In the next moment, Mrs. Mitchell grabbed my arm, pulling me away from the plane.

Shouts of "Godspeed" erupted from the small crowd of family and well-wishers, then the little dragonfly roared into action. Blustery snow churned in its wake as the plane rolled down the snow-covered strip and then lifted into the air — the roar of the engine now drowning out the roar of the crowd.

I watched Mrs. May, who never stopped waving until the plane was a tiny speck in the grey sky. Beside me, Mrs. Mitchell scolded on and on about my outrageous behaviour and how they should never have brought me there, but I let her words disappear into the snowy wind. Maybe the bars and the encouraging words wouldn't make a difference, but at least I did something. At least I tried.

As I turned my attention from the sky, I barely ducked in time to miss a snowball that whizzed by my head. "Look out!" I yelled, too late as the snowball smacked Helen's head.

She screamed and rubbed the back of her head with her mitt. "I'm telling my father," she shrieked through the driving snow, but the culprit wasn't paying any attention to her.

"Who's the idiot throwing the snowballs?" I asked.

"That's Kenny Wilson. He's as big as a house and meaner than a rabid dog."

I scooped up a handful of snow and formed it into a perfect ball. Snowballs were not my area of expertise, but I had a pretty good arm for softball. I fired it as hard as I could at the unsuspecting Kenny, who was now laughing with his buddies.

"Ow!" The snowball caught Kenny in the open space between his jacket and his toque. He swung around and gaped at us as though he couldn't believe it.

"Did you see the look on his face?" Helen shouted with glee.

Mrs. Mitchell gave me a swift look of disapproval and wasted no time in ending the snowball fight by telling everyone it was time to leave.

"Who taught you to throw like that?" Helen asked, as we walked across the field to where the car was parked.

"Just a lucky shot," I said, but I was pretty proud of myself.

"He's madder than a wet hen," Helen said. Then her face turned serious. "I sure hope he doesn't think I threw it. Otherwise, I'm done for."

"Bullies need a taste of their own medicine every now and then," I said.

CHAPTER 7

A Friend

WARMING MY FEET BY the hot stove, I pulled my cellphone out of my pocket. No signal. Of course. Not that I needed further evidence that I had really left the twenty-first century. Standing in the bitter snowstorm at Blatchford Field had done that effectively enough.

"What's that?" Helen asked, as she stirred the hot cocoa on the stove.

"A useless piece of plastic, apparently," I said, shoving it back in my pocket.

"Plastic? Let me see that thing."

I showed it to her briefly, but then changed the subject.

"What do you think they're saying?" Mr. and Mrs. Mitchell were in the living room discussing the "situation," which is how they referred to me.

Helen poured the cocoa into mugs for us. "They are saying that they've never seen a black kangaroo hood with sparkles on it like that."

I looked down at my hoodie with the glitter star in the middle and then at Helen's hand-knitted blue sweater with the white snowflake in the centre. Yeah, maybe, but I had the feeling that Mrs. Mitchell had a few choice words about me that had nothing to do with my clothing.

"It's quite a peculiar thing to do," Helen continued, "sneaking into someone's house like that."

"I didn't *sneak* in. I *ran* in, thinking this was my house."

"Well, *that*," Helen said, "is pecuuuuuliar, if you ask me. Who wouldn't know what house they live in?"

"Okay. I'll give you that. But trust me, I did not want to run into your house. I wanted to run into the house that used to belong to my grandparents and I can't help it that you were here."

"You talk funny and you don't make any sense, but I will be your friend because I don't know *anyone* who has hit Kenny Wilson with a snowball." She smiled.

"Thanks." That was something at least.

Helen looked thoughtful for a moment. "You know, if you told me the truth, I wouldn't snitch on you."

"What if I tell you the truth, and then you think I'm not

telling the truth, and you tell your parents, and I get into even more trouble?"

"What if you tell me the truth and I promise I won't tell a soul? I swear. Cross my heart and hope to die." She made a flourishing cross over her chest.

"Okay, but I just want to say that if I was going to make something up, I wouldn't be creative enough, let alone crazy enough to make up something like what you're going to hear. Just keep that in mind." I took a deep breath and then began. Really, what did I have to lose?

Helen's eyes grew wide as I told about my experience at the New Year's Eve party and then at the library, but surprisingly, she didn't interrupt.

"The thing I can't figure out," Helen said when I finished, "is how you sound mostly normal, not crazy at all."

"Normal is overrated," I said, resting my head on my hands. Suddenly, I was completely exhausted.

"What else did I write in my journal?" Helen asked, as if it were a test.

"You said that this will be the most perfect year, because you will turn thirteen, and your mother said that you would be able to get your hair cut into a bob like your cousin Elizabeth," I quoted with little enthusiasm.

"You *did* read my journal ... or maybe you're a mind-reader, like Madame Zena at the circus. That's just the strangest thing ever."

Mr. and Mrs. Mitchell came into the kitchen just then.

"We've made some inquiries as to what to do in such a situation, and I must say that you have put us in quite a co-nundrum, young lady." Mrs. Mitchell's icy blue eyes bored fiercely into mine. "If you have any further information that would assist us in finding your family, you'd best be forth-right about it and stop this foolishness."

An awkward silence followed. What could I offer by way of explanation or solution? And so I said nothing.

Mrs. Mitchell's forehead furrowed into a scowl. "I'm wait-ing for a return call from Judge Murphy, and then a decision will be made. We won't turn you out into a snowstorm, but you'd best mind your p's and q's."

⌒

Helen and I had just finished putting away the last plate from supper dishes when Mr. Mitchell called from the front room. "Come on, girls, the broadcast will be on any minute now."

Helen and I sat on the rug facing the very large radio. It was odd not having a screen to look at. First there was a short jingle about some vegetable tablets that cured everything from ingrown toenails to indigestion, and then the announc-er's voice crackled through the wires.

> You're listening to CJCA. We interrupt the regularly scheduled programming to bring you this special update of what is now being called the Mission of Mercy. Excite-ment is building across the country as word of this amaz-ing flight spreads. Captain Wilfrid May, known to many

as "Wop," and his buddy Vic Horner left Blatchford Field in Edmonton, this afternoon, braving extreme weather conditions.

"We were there," Helen whispered excitedly.

"I know. I can hardly believe it."

For those of you who haven't heard yet, these fearless men are delivering a diphtheria antidote serum to the north-ern community of Little Red River, where there has been a confirmed case of diphtheria. Knowing they were in a race against the clock with this villain, Dr. Hammond contacted Captain May about the possibility of flying the life-saving serum to them. An open-cockpit biplane and horrible weather is not the best recipe for a pleasant flight, but it would take more than frigid temperatures and poor visibility to deter the courageous Captain May who faced the infamous Red Baron and lived to tell the tale. Yes, siree!

"Dad, could you tell us the story of the Red Baron?" Helen asked.

"Shush," Mr. Mitchell said, not taking his eyes off the radio. "Stop interrupting."

It just so happened that at McLennan Junction, some men were following the flight on their crystal radio sets. One of the men figured that McLennan Junction would be on their flight path. He and his buddies cleared a land-ing field in case the pilots couldn't make it all the way to

Peace River. Imagine the shouts and cheers rising from the crew on the ground as they frantically waved to their heroes in the sky. Was the runway wide enough? Long enough? Had they done a good enough job for the little Avian to land? It appeared that all the hard work was for ·nought as the little plane flew right past. But then, the tiny plane dipped down and circled back, and the weary pilots landed on the McLennan Junction runway!

What a story we are witnessing. Yes siree! A story about angels on the ground, and heroes in the air. That's all for now, folks. Keep those radio stations tuned to CJCA as we bring you up-to-the-minute coverage of this heroic Mission of Mercy.

Mr. Mitchell rose and turned off the radio. "Well, if that isn't something. Glad they made it safely so far and that they didn't try to push on to Peace River. We all better say a prayer for our boys of the air. There's still a long way to go before they're safely home."

"As for the news on the ground," Mrs. Mitchell announced, "I spoke with Judge Murphy who suggested that, if we are willing, then keeping Kami here for the time being is probably for the best. Mrs. Bell from the Children's Aid Society already has her hands full, and there simply isn't anyone available on such short notice."

Helen cheered and I felt a flood of relief. "But," Mrs. Mitchell continued, "there will be no highjinks. Is that understood?"

"Yes, Ma'am," Helen shouted.

"Thank you," I said. "I won't be any trouble."

"I'm not finished," Mrs. Mitchell continued. "Kami, you will go to school with Helen in the morning. By the time school is over, we'll have some answers."

The only answer I wanted was why I was still here.

CHAPTER 8

The School Bully

"OW." I WOKE UP abruptly with a foot pressing on my ribs.

"Oops. I forgot you were there," Helen said, pulling her foot back onto the bed.

The realization that I was still in Helen's house hit me like a blast of cold air. "What am I going to do?" I whispered under my breath. This couldn't be happening.

"Hop to it, girls." Mrs. Mitchell bustled into the room, her arms full of clothes, which she dumped on Helen's bed. "Luckily for Kami, your Aunt Kate brought over Elizabeth's hand-me-downs last week, and I found some things that will do nicely for school."

School. I hadn't really thought I'd be here for school, and I wasn't looking forward to it. If only Mrs. Mitchell would let me stay home, I might be able to figure out how to get out of here.

"No dilly-dallying. Breakfast is on the table."

"I wouldn't mind helping out around the house this morning," I suggested eagerly to Mrs. Mitchell. "The school won't be expecting me."

She paused for a moment, and I dared to hope she'd agree to the idea.

"No," she shook her head firmly. "I can't have you underfoot this morning. You'll go to school with Helen." And that was that.

"It won't be so bad," Helen said, as she scurried out the door to the bathroom.

Miserable and frustrated, I pulled a sailor top off the stack of clothes and put it on. Oh my gosh. Was I really going to have to go out in public in this? Reluctantly, I stepped into the matching navy skirt, which was too big around the waist and draped crookedly over my hips. Perfect. I was holding up one long navy stocking deciding what to do with it when Helen came back in the room.

"How do these stay up?" I asked.

Helen stared at me for a moment, then made a sour face. "Why do you ask silly questions like that, pretending you've never seen stockings before? It's not funny, you know."

"You got that right," I said. Helen wasn't the only one in a bad mood this morning.

I picked up a pair of bloomers, which went under the skirt. Gosh. So many clothes. Lying at the bottom of the stack was a white belt thing with four clips dangling from elastics. You've got to be kidding. I watched Helen out of the corner of my eye and sure enough, she was clipping the stockings, front and back, to the white belt that she had fastened around her waist. I never thought of tights as an invention, but now they seemed like a brilliant idea.

Finally I had everything on, and the result was not pretty. Between the goofy sailor top and the too-big skirt, I felt like a giant toddler in hand-me-downs. Thank goodness I wouldn't know anyone at the school.

"Hurry up, your porridge is getting cold," Mrs. Mitchell said as we entered the kitchen. "What took you so long?"

"Kami had a bit of trouble with Cousin Elizabeth's clothes." Helen pointed to the sloppy skirt. "They *are* kind of big."

"Could I wear my own clothes?" I asked, but this earned me a fierce glare.

"You look fine," Helen's mother insisted. "Now eat your porridge so that you're not late."

I ate a spoonful of the colourless oatmeal that was similar, I imagined, to eating bits of cardboard soaked in warm water. Helen was shovelling it in as if it were apple pie, so I made my best effort to get it down.

After breakfast, Mrs. Mitchell handed me a canvas sack with a few school supplies and a note for the headmaster. Then Helen and I bundled up for the icy walk to the school. Although the sun was shining, I was relieved when we reached the large brick building. At the edge of the fenced yard, a group of girls skipped over to us, arms linked.

"Hello, Helen," they chimed in their sing-songy voices. Then they pointed at me and burst out laughing before skipping off again.

"Don't pay any attention to them. My friend Hattie isn't like that." Helen scanned the schoolyard, looking for her friend. "Sometimes she has to stay home to watch her twin brothers. Her mother is going to have another baby soon."

When the bell rang, I followed Helen into line. That's when I noticed the word GIRLS stamped in concrete, above the entrance. "This door is only for girls?"

"Of course. The boy's side of the yard is over there." Helen pointed to the opposite side of the school. "It wouldn't make any sense for them to come in this door."

"The boys have their own side of the playground?"

Helen laughed. "Of course. Who'd want to play in the boy's yard? It would be awful." She stuck out her tongue.

I wondered what other surprises I was in for today.

"I'm in Mr. Green's class," Helen said, as we walked through the doors and up a few stairs to the main floor. "He's really strict, but maybe he'll let you sit with me since Hattie isn't here today. Then I can kind of show you what to do."

Helen's classroom was just past the office. Whispers filled the air as I hung my coat on the hook beside Helen's in what she called the cloak room. Everyone seemed to think I was Chinese, but I couldn't be bothered correcting them. If there were any Japanese people living in Edmonton, they weren't living around these parts, obviously. Anyway, I didn't plan to stick around long enough for it to matter. At least the sailor suit was not as bad as I thought it would be. Judging from the other girls, the sailor-look was a big deal right now.

When we entered the room, I saw what Helen meant by us sitting together. The bench seats, which were attached to the front of the desk table behind you, were made for two people.

Mr. Green stood at the front of the room, peering down at his students over the top of his half-moon glasses. The walls were bare with the exception of a photograph of the King, with a gold plate that said, KING GEORGE V. The blackboard, on the other hand, was filled with yellow chalk instructions from top to bottom, without space for so much as another punctuation mark.

Mr. Green paced across the platform, tapping his pencil on the class attendance list. In his greenish suit, with wisps of fluffy pale hair springing from the top of his head, he reminded me of a giant celery stalk with glasses.

Helen and I approached him with the note. "I'm staying with the Mitchells," I began to explain.

"Speak when spoken to," he snapped, taking the note. His brows puckered as he read. Then he folded the note and peered over his glasses. "You're Kami Anderson?"

I nodded, keeping my mouth firmly closed this time.

"Speak, when you are spoken to," he snapped again. "We have manners in this classroom."

"Yes," I answered, not liking the Celery Stalk at all.

"Yes, sir!" He insisted.

"Yes, sir," I repeated dutifully, while Helen scurried to her seat.

"*Anderson?* I've never heard of a Chinese family named Anderson," he announced loudly as though addressing the entire class. Snickers rippled through the room.

My face grew hot and I felt my ears turning red. I wanted to correct him, but said nothing. Instead I stood awkwardly in front of the class, not sure what I was supposed to do. Finally he told me to go and sit with Helen. "She brought you here. It will be her job to keep you in line until recess. We'll figure out what to do about you at that time." Helen smiled weakly, and I was sure she was having second thoughts about me being in her class. It was not a great start.

I had barely taken my seat when a single note sounded from a little instrument that Mr. Green blew into, and the entire class stood at attention. Everyone began to sing "God Save the King." I knew some of the words, but felt Helen's elbow in my ribs when I sang *Queen* by accident.

When the class sat down, Mr. Green asked if any students had heard about the Mission of Mercy and the heroic flight of the pilots. Helen's hand shot up immediately. She stood when the teacher called on her, and shared in great detail about seeing the pilots off on this special mission.

"They have a little charcoal burner in the back in order to keep the diphtheria serum from freezing," she said with an important smile. I felt myself breathe normally again. Finally, the focus had shifted away from me.

After the rough start, I concentrated extra hard on the assignments. Reading was easy and then there were some arithmetic drills. Even I was surprised at how well I did without a calculator. The word problem on the board, however, was another story. It wasn't complicated but I had no idea what *bushels* and *pecks* were. I was about to ask Helen when the teacher walked by.

"Well, well, well, it looks like Princess Ming doesn't know everything after all," he said, looking pleased.

Penmanship was worse. I had spent very little time learning to write cursive in school, and this particular brand had more loops and curls than the wool on a baby lamb. But the fountain pen was the biggest problem. It blobbed nonstop and eventually quit working all together. I watched the boy across the aisle fill his and it didn't look that hard. First, I opened the little clip on the side and slid the nib into the jar of ink, but then Helen accidentally bumped my elbow and the entire bottle of ink went flying.

"Kami Anderson," Mr. Green shouted, "you are completely exasperating. Do you thrive on being difficult, or have you never been to school before?" He opened a cupboard at the back of the room and pulled out a rag. "Perhaps you will know how to use this?" Helen rushed to help me, but by this time I was really, really not liking Mr. Green.

When the recess bell rang, I made a decision. I would not

be returning to the classroom. I'd tell Mrs. Mitchell I was sick if I had to, but I was done with this school experience. I filled the sack with the borrowed supplies and put on the oversized coat.

"What are you doing? It's recess," Helen said, reaching for her coat.

"Shush," I whispered, pressing my finger against my lips. I didn't want to talk about it with the Celery Stalk within hearing distance. We left the cloakroom and had just stepped into the hall when someone smacked into me from behind. As I turned, the hulk of a kid who threw the snowball at the airfield spat in my face.

Disgusted, I wiped my face on my sleeve. "Coward," I yelled to his back.

Helen gasped in disbelief. She wasn't the only one. Others in the hallway stopped and stared at the newcomer who was stupid enough to antagonize the biggest kid in the school.

"You talking to someone, China girl?" The hefty boy turned and folded his arms.

Helen grabbed my arm. "Now you've done it. Let's go. Hurry, before Kenny flattens you."

But I wasn't about to back down now. That jerk needed to be taught a lesson, and I was crazy-mad enough to want to teach it.

A hostile grin on his face, Kenny swaggered down the hall in my direction. I dropped the canvas bag, and shrugged out of the coat, but I did not take my eyes off him for a second. When he got close, he reached for my hair. In one swift motion my arm came up to block him, then I pivoted and snapped my leg out above my head kicking him squarely in the face with every ounce of fury that had built up inside me. This was a favourite move of mine from martial arts class, and one I had perfected. I moved with lightning speed and the opponent never expected it.

Kenny shouted choice words at me as blood spurted from his nose like a fountain. A stunned silence followed. For the first time that morning, I saw something resembling admiration in the eyes of the crowd around me.

I put on the coat and picked the bag up off the floor, but it was already too late.

"March," Mr. Green barked, pointing me in the direction of the office. Kenny had disappeared rather quickly, I noticed. I was instructed to sit facing the secretary whose job it was, apparently, to scowl at me and tsk, tsk under her breath. Mr. Green rapped sharply on the frosted glass door that said HEADMASTER in bold black letters, and soon disappeared behind it.

This whole situation was ridiculous. I had never ever been in trouble at school before, but this teacher was nuts. I should have ignored Kenny and left this crazy place when I had the chance. Still, I had to admit, it was pretty sweet to see the stunned look on Kenny's face when he realized a girl had got the better of him.

Finally the door opened and Mr. Green reappeared. "Headmaster Graves is ready to see you now. I don't think I'll be seeing you back in the classroom." His smirk was annoying, but I was too worried about what would happen now to care.

"Be seated." The headmaster closed the door behind me and gestured to the straight-back chair opposite the polished mahogany desk. "I spoke with Mr. Green in order to gain some understanding of the situation," he began. "He described you as an unruly, disrespectful student, who has now kicked and injured one of our students. A student, I may add, whose father donates to our school on a regular basis. We do not tolerate such behaviour at our school."

"That boy spat in my face and was about to hit me," I blurted. "I was only defending myself. And Mr. Green doesn't like me because I'm Japanese."

This little speech did not impress Headmaster Graves. His face turned red, and he puffed himself up like a porcupine on the attack.

"How dare you insult the teachers and the students of this school." Angrily, he shook his finger in my face. "You are an insolent child, who has obviously not been taught respect for those in positions of authority."

"I didn't start it."

"Further discussion is not necessary. You are not a student at this school and should not have been allowed to stay. Mrs. Roberts, in the front office, is contacting the Mitchells to come and get you at this very moment. You should not have attended this school today, but you did. And you behaved badly. It is my unpleasant task, therefore, to teach you a lesson in manners. Stand up."

I stood, but instinctively took a step back. The headmaster took a strip of leather out of his desk drawer and told me to hold out both hands. What? Then I realized that he actually intended to hit me with this piece of leather that folded into a handle at one end. Before he could repeat his command, I opened the door and flew out of the office. I could hear the secretary and the headmaster both yelling at me as I raced through the hallway, down the stairs and out into the school-yard.

The headmaster yelled out the door to some boys to stop me from leaving the yard, but nobody moved until I was safely out of the schoolyard. As much as they didn't like me, it appeared they disliked Kenny even more.

I didn't stop running until the house was in sight. Then I slowed a little and tried to catch my breath. Tears melted tracks down my frozen cheeks as I made my way along the path to the front door.

CHAPTER 9

The Judge

WHEN MRS. MITCHELL answered the door, the fire in her eyes dissolved any courage I had rallied when facing the bully. She opened the door to let me in, but it wasn't hard to tell she had already got a phone call.

"Less than one day at school and already you have shown yourself to be disrespectful and ungrateful," Mrs. Mitchell accused. "I can't say that I'm surprised, but I didn't think it was too much to ask you to make it through one day without disgracing us."

"I was defending myself," I said, swallowing the lump in my throat.

"Save your story for the judge. I've heard the entire account from Headmaster Graves, and that's all I care to know about the matter. I am deeply disappointed."

"Judge? I didn't break the law."

"Mr. Mitchell is coming home from the newspaper office to drive us to the courthouse. Sit on the bench in the cloak-room until he arrives."

What now? I had no idea that Mrs. Mitchell would be so angry that I put the bully in his place. Not that I'd given it a lot of thought. I was too busy thinking about how good it would feel to best that arrogant bully. Now it didn't seem like such a good idea. Well, it wouldn't happen again. I'd be per-fectly behaved from now on, no matter what.

Mrs. Mitchell slid into her muskrat coat and matching fur hat. "Considering the aggressive nature of your personality, Judge Murphy agreed to meet with us immediately. It will be up to the judge as to your proper placement in the event that your parents cannot be located."

I blinked my eyes rapidly several times, not wanting to cry. If Mom were in this situation, she wouldn't cry. She would figure something out. What was it she always said to me? I closed my eyes and tried to hear her voice. *There are no big problems, Kami. Only a lot of little problems piled one on top of the other. You don't have to solve them all at once. Start with one little problem. Solve that first, and then solve the next one. Before you know it, your big problem is just one little problem. You can solve one little problem, can't you Kami?* That was Mom for you. Nothing too big to solve.

It wasn't long before Mr. Mitchell pulled up in Lizzie. I

wrapped the scarf around my face and went out the door. "There's a blanket for you," he said, opening the back door.

Perched on the frozen seat, I felt my stomach churning into knots. What if they sent me away somewhere?

Lizzie careened all over the place on the icy trails and then one of the wheels got stuck in a rut. Mr. Mitchell pulled on the gas lever, which shot the car into a chunk of ice, bouncing me to the roof. It was a miracle that the wheels didn't fly off in different directions, and us with them. Mrs. Mitchell muttered that she should have driven the auto herself at the rate he was going. I was thinking Lizzie was an accident waiting to happen, no matter who was driving.

"If the judge speaks to you," Mrs. Mitchell said, now that Lizzie was on all four wheels again, "you must answer 'Yes, Your Honour,' or 'No, Your Honour.' There is to be no disrespect. Is that clear?"

"Yes." I stared out the front, dreading this whole event. Mrs. Mitchell really thought I was rude and difficult, which probably wasn't going to help my situation with the judge.

By the time we reached Jasper Avenue, excited sounds of the city rose from every direction. Car horns honked at slow-moving pedestrians, screeching tires skidded to a stop against the sidewalk, newspaper vendors hawked their papers, men in wagons yelled at hesitant horses, and streetcars rattled through the centre of everything.

It was a whole new city to the one that had recently greeted Mom and me. Proud new buildings lined both sides of the wide Jasper Avenue, each one flaunting its unique personality. Banks displayed elegant pillars, stores hid behind leisurely awnings, and stately brick buildings showed off their decorative concrete detailing with arched windows. Reigning over all of them, was the one familiar landmark — the Macdonald Hotel.

Lizzie clunked to a stop in front of a handsome sandstone building with tall pillars at the entrance.

"This is our stop," Mr. Mitchell said, holding the door for me.

Mr. and Mrs. Mitchell talked in hushed voices as we entered the right side of the matching double entrances. According to the security guard, Magistrate Murphy was not in court at the moment, but Mrs. Mitchell was well aware of this fact. She also knew precisely where to find the judge among the myriad of offices. Mrs. Mitchell was the type of person who knew everything without being told. The clicking of her boots echoed through the marble halls as we wound our way past offices and rooms furnished in velvet and gleaming wood. The offices looked more like old-fashioned parlours with their rich burgundy carpets and gilt-framed paintings. We stopped at a small, rather plain office, and Mrs. Mitchell knocked on the open door announcing our arrival.

The woman looked up from behind a stack of file folders, revealing a pleasant, welcoming face. There was something familiar about her, but I couldn't quite figure out what it was.

"Good morning, Your Honour," Mrs. Mitchell greeted the woman. "Thank you for fitting us in."

Your Honour? That's when I noticed the black robe and white collar hanging on a coat tree in the corner. A woman judge, in 1929? That was a surprise.

The woman rose from her chair and shook hands with Mr. and Mrs. Mitchell. She was more sturdy than beautiful, but she carried herself regally, with an air of importance. And although the firm set to her jaw gave the impression she was a no-nonsense type, her eyes, when they met mine, were warm.

"Hello Millie, Jack. Please call me Emily. We are friends, so there's no need to hold with the formalities. I want to assure you that you have done the right thing in bringing the girl to me. I deal with these young women all the time."

Emily? Emily Murphy? You've got to be kidding. No wonder she looked familiar. I had seen her picture in my seventh-grade Social Studies text book when we studied famous Canadians. This judge. This woman judge from 1929 had to be Emily Murphy. *The* Emily Murphy. She had been the first female magistrate in the entire British Empire and an activist for women's rights. Wow. This was crazy.

"Have you seen a spirit, young lady?" Magistrate Murphy asked, her head held high, like a queen.

"I'm very happy to meet you," I blurted out eagerly. "I've never met anyone famous before."

Mrs. Mitchell smothered a cough behind her gloves but I could see that Mr. Mitchell was smiling.

"Famous, am I?" Magistrate Murphy said. "And how is that?"

"We learned in school about the Persons Case and how you were the leader with those other four women, to get the BNA Act changed. You're the first female police magistrate in all of the British Empire and you wrote a lot of books under the name Janey Canuck." I stopped to take a breath.

"I'm taken aback, I must say, that you are so well-versed in my life, especially with regards to the Persons case, which is only now before the Privy Council. How interesting that you rhymed this off as a completed deed, when the outcome is still to be determined."

"Really?" I asked, surprised at this information. "But you must know that it will pass."

"Your Honour, Emily," Mrs. Mitchell interrupted. "While no one would argue with your significant contributions to society, surely you can see that this girl is trying to manipulate the situation to her advantage."

"You may be right, but don't you think she is doing a marvellous job of it?" Judge Murphy chuckled and Mr. Mitchell laughed out loud.

"Kami Anderson." The judge looked at notes on her desk. "Anderson is a good Scottish name. Are you aware of that?"

"Yes, Your Honour, I am. My grandfather was born in Scotland, but my father was born in Edmonton, and so was I."

"Well, Kami Anderson, I appreciate your enthusiastic endorsement. However, according to Mrs. Mitchell, you were not so gracious in your behaviour at school today. Tell me what happened."

"I can tell you precisely what happened," Mrs. Mitchell snapped. "I heard it straight from the headmaster."

"Yes, Millie, I got the details from you over the telephone," Magistrate Murphy said, "but I feel that it's only fair to let the girl tell her side of the story. It has been my experience that there are two sides to every story."

I began at the start of the school day, not wanting to miss anything. Mrs. Murphy's face didn't betray her thoughts, but I hoped she would be more reasonable than Mrs. Mitchell had been.

"Mr. Green should have brought that Kenny brute to the office is what he should have done," Mr. Mitchell said. "He's a terror at that school and Headmaster Graves knows it." Then he looked at me, a serious expression on his face. "The headmaster was well within his rights, you know, to discipline you for breaking the rules. I don't hold with giving girls the strap, but you shouldn't have run away like that. He can't run a school with everyone doing whatever they please." He paused for a moment. "Did you really kick that big oaf, Kenny, and make his nose bleed? I would like to have seen that."

"Jack," Mrs. Mitchell shrilled. "This girl is obviously troubled. It's not right for you to encourage her that way."

Emily Murphy cleared her throat as though reminding the Mitchells why they were here. "This is what I propose. Let me look into the situation a little more thoroughly. If none of my searches for a missing girl result in any satisfactory solution, we will have no choice but to make her a ward of the court."

A ward of the court? I had heard of foster children being wards of the court, or children who were victims of abuse. But it hadn't dawned on me before that I could be made a ward of the court. Oh my gosh. No matter what, I could not let that happen.

"At this time, I see no evidence of a violent personality," Emily Murphy was saying. "I know that there can be problems with the oriental people, and as a result there are several avenues I will need to pursue." The magistrate turned to face me directly. "Kami, are you willing to cooperate completely, with no further outbursts such as you had at school today?"

"Yes." As much as I disagreed with the question, I knew that was the right answer.

Mrs. Mitchell's lips pressed into a tight line. "I'm sure Kami appreciates what you are doing for her."

"If it's temporary, I don't see why she couldn't stay with us," Mr. Mitchell suggested. My hopes rose. *Please.* I silently begged Mrs. Mitchell, but already her eyes were popping out of her head at the suggestion.

"Kami has promised there will be no further problems such as the one that arose today. What do you say, Millie? Would you be willing to have her as a domestic until we can sort through some information? Her room and board would be covered so it would be at no added expense to you."

"Emily," Mrs. Mitchell began, her voice cool and crisp.

"Surely you understand that she can't stay with us. Not after everything that has happened."

"I'll behave. I promise," I blurted out. "My mother won't know where I am if you place me somewhere else."

"I like a girl that's got a bit of spunk and stands up for herself," Mr. Mitchell stated, "and you could use the help. It would give you more time to write real articles for the paper. You'd like that."

"This is not about a writing career for me, Jack." Mrs. Mitchell gripped the gloves tightly in her hand. "You know I rarely go against your wishes, but I am absolutely firm on this matter. We have Helen to consider. Doesn't Children's Aid have someone who can take her?" Mrs. Mitchell asked.

"You have made your position clear," Emily Murphy stated. "She is now my responsibility and no longer of concern to you. You can trust me to take care of the details."

"I'll see you next Thursday at the Press Club meeting, Emily," Mrs. Mitchell called over her shoulder. And then they were gone.

When the Mitchells walked through that door, it was like being told you can never go home. I didn't know what to do, and my brain refused to work. Sheer terror occupied every corner of my mind.

CHAPTER 10

Miss Evelyn

"IF YOU WOULD SIMPLY tell the truth, we could settle this matter much more quickly," Judge Murphy said after the Mitchells left. She opened her desk drawer and took out a file folder. "This woman is in need of a domestic, but you are a trifle young for this particular situation." She continued to page through the documents in the folder.

"You're finding me a job?" I began to shiver uncontrollably. "I'm only thirteen."

"Do you not work with your mother sometimes?"

"No. I go to school," I answered, the meaning of the question gradually sinking in. "My mother is a professional."

"In which profession does your mother work?"

"She works with architects and engineers to design cities."

"Your mother designs cities." Mrs. Murphy's face sagged, like I was sucking all the energy out of her.

What was I thinking? A woman who designs cities in 1929, would be like a woman who takes a space bus to work on Mars, in 2004.

"When did you arrive in Edmonton?"

"I was born in Edmonton but we moved to Vancouver when I was six. We only arrived back in Edmonton yesterday."

"And you don't know where your mother is?"

I shook my head. "I have no idea how to contact her."

"Your mother designs cities," Mrs. Murphy repeated, "and you just moved here from Vancouver." I nodded. "But you have no idea where your mother is."

This was not going well. Obviously the situation called for a little creative storytelling, not the bald truth, and I had failed miserably.

"You are a conundrum. There's no denying that." Mrs. Murphy paused, coughing into a white hankie. "I have dealt with a lot of young women in my twelve years as police magistrate, but I have never come across anyone quite like you. This would be a lot easier if you weren't so articulate and bright."

She asked me to wait in the hall while she made some phone calls. I hovered outside the door, hoping to catch some of the conversation but not even a mumble came through the heavy wood door. Finally I settled into one of the straight-back chairs lining the hall, and stared at the closed door.

Moments later, Mrs. Murphy appeared, dressed in a black wool coat, a furry animal of some sort draped around her shoulders. She was carrying a large black briefcase.

"Come with me," she said, closing the door behind her. "Fortunately, I'm not scheduled in court this afternoon."

Was there an orphanage or some other place where she planned to drop me off? My stomach clenched into a tight ball. Mrs. Murphy coughed like crazy as we walked along Jasper Avenue, so I didn't ask any questions. At the end of the block, we caught the trolley, which was heading to the university, according to the sign. As we bumped along, Mrs. Murphy filled me in on the plan.

"Given the gravity of the situation, I have decided to take you in, until we acquire a proper placement for you."

"I'm going to your house?" This was better than I had dared hope for.

"Only until I find you a suitable place," she emphasized.

"What would make a suitable placement?" I asked, hoping this did not sound rude.

The judge cocked her head to one side, choosing her words carefully.

"The Children's Aid Society usually finds homes for orphans and children who cannot live with their parents for one reason or another, but there is a shortage of foster homes at the moment. You are not a typical case, by any means, so we need to look at other options. As you pointed out, you are too young to be sent out to work, although that, too, is a consideration, given the right situation."

"What do you mean by *other options*?" I asked, not sure that I wanted to hear the answer.

"Goodness child, you have far too many questions. You must trust me to find a suitable solution. That may take a little time. Until then, you will be trained as a domestic under the supervision of my daughter, Evelyn."

"Thank you." At least I wasn't going to an orphanage. Despite her stern voice, I felt that Mrs. Murphy was someone I could trust. That gave me a tiny ray of hope. Another cause for hope was that, as the trolley rolled across the bridge, crossing the river, I realized that we were going back toward Helen's house.

"My home is in very close proximity to the university," Mrs. Murphy said. "That's always been my favourite part of the city." .

It was my favourite part, too. If Emily Murphy's house was close to the university, then it couldn't be too far from Helen's house either. We got off the trolley and walked for a couple of blocks to a two-storey house resembling a box standing on end. Brown shingles covered the entire top storey like an ugly brown hat. Not the elegant home you'd expect for a judge.

A woman wearing an apron and sensible brown shoes met us at the door. "Mother, don't tell me you've brought home another girl to assist with the housework." Her face creased into a sharp frown.

So this was Evelyn. *Miss Evelyn* to me, I was informed.

Miss Evelyn looked kind of old to be living with her parents, I thought.

"The girl has had a difficult day," Mrs. Murphy told her daughter, as she hung her coat on the coat tree in the corner. "Settle her into the maid's room and find her a bite to eat. Then you can work out what her duties will be."

I slipped off my coat and hung it beside Mrs. Murphy's, thinking this was a helpful thing to do. But Miss Evelyn swept the coat from the hook and motioned for me to follow her. She took me to a tiny room off the kitchen. The room was the size of a broom closet, but the bed looked soft and I longed to curl up in a ball and sleep. Miss Evelyn had other plans.

"You will earn your keep," she informed me as I washed my hands at the kitchen sink, "until such time as Mother finds you a permanent placement." She gestured for me to sit at the round table in the centre of the kitchen. "When you are finished your tea, we'll go over your duties." She set out a thick slice of bread and a jar of jam. My stomach was still jittery, but once I took the first bite of homemade bread, I realized how hungry I was.

Miss Evelyn, I soon discovered, was picky even for a perfectionist. After the evening meal, when I was asked to "set the kitchen to rights," nothing I did met with approval. You would think washing dishes would be fairly straightforward, but Miss Evelyn made it into a science. Holy Hannah! Washing, rinsing, drying, putting-away, all required systematic precision. Glassware, silverware, china, pots and pans. That was the order. And then there was the scrubbing of the counter and the mopping of the floor. No crumb escaped Miss Evelyn's eagle eyes.

In between cleaning instructions, Miss Evelyn filled me in on other rules and expectations. Mr. Murphy, for example, was not a *Mr.* at all because of his clergyman status with the Church of England. He should be addressed as Reverend Murphy, although many of the congregation referred to him simply as *the Reverend*. His wife nicknamed him Padre.

We were just finishing up in the kitchen when the Reverend called from the living room. "The Mission of Mercy broadcast is about to start, folks."

"Oh, I wonder if the pilots have made it with the medicine," I said, excited to hear what was happening.

Miss Evelyn scowled. "You are not a guest here, nor are you family," she was quick to point out. "It will be the same at every home in which you are placed. As far as I am concerned, Mother takes her work far too personally. I discourage her from bringing girls home, but she believes in giving young women a chance." She wagged her finger at me to emphasize her point. "Consider yourself fortunate and don't abuse her generous nature by expecting to join the family."

That was that. I filled my wash pitcher with water from the pot on the stove, the way Miss Evelyn had shown me, and was about to go into my room when the Reverend came into the kitchen.

"Hurry up, you'll miss the broadcast," he said, taking a bowl of powdery white mints out of the cupboard.

"Miss Evelyn thought it wouldn't be appropriate," I said, setting the heavy pitcher on the table, "for me to join the family, I mean."

"Did she now. Well, considering this is a significant historical event, I think we could break the rules just this once." Then he bent down and whispered. "Her bark is worse than her bite. I'll manage Evelyn for you." He tilted his head toward the parlour, gesturing for me to follow him.

I left the pitcher on the table and quickly caught up to Reverend Murphy in case he changed his mind.

"I invited Miss Kami to join us this evening, Evelyn," the Reverend said. "I told her you wouldn't mind because this is such an historical and educational broadcast."

"Good idea, Padre," Mrs. Murphy said, her voice sounding a little gravelly. The Reverend turned the knob on the radio to turn up the volume.

> *Hello all you people out in radio land. You're listening to CJCA where it's our mission to keep you informed about the famous Mission of Mercy.*

> *Today in Peace River, around noon, the Avro Avian landed on the cleared river ice as planned. The pilots refuelled and prepared for the last stretch of the journey. As the plane took off, fighter-pilot Wop May realized that they weren't going to clear the railway bridge over the river, and before you could say "Look out boys," the plane swooped under the bridge, then soared up and away on the other side. Atta boy, Wop! And now, a word from our sponsors.*

Mrs. Murphy's chest heaved as she expelled a sharp cough, which triggered a series of machine-gun-like coughs.

"You're sounding poorly tonight, Cookie," her husband commented.

"Bit of a tickle in my throat is all," Mrs. Murphy croaked between coughs.

I wondered if I should offer to get her a glass of water, but just then the advertising jingle ended and the announcer came back on.

> Our brave knights of the air followed the river to Fort Vermillion. Exhausted, and near frozen solid, they handed over the medicine to Dr. Hammond who, with the help of his horse and sleigh, raced the life-saving cargo over ice and snow, fifty miles back to Little Red River where he would begin administering the crucial serum.
>
> Stay tuned tomorrow, folks, for further details of the Mission of Mercy. As soon as we know when to expect our heroes home, we'll be the first to let you know. But for now, our love and prayers will follow them. Good night folks.

The Reverend switched off the radio and announced he was turning in for the night. "You'd better ring Dr. Berry about that cough," he told his wife, helping her out of her chair. "No working tonight."

"Ah, Padre, I'm a tough old bird. You know that," Mrs. Murphy spluttered between coughs.

"My grandma swears by ginger tea for any kind of cold or cough," I said. "She used to say it could raise the dead it was so powerful. I could make you some if you have ginger root."

"Kami . . ." Miss Evelyn began.

"Never mind, Evelyn. She's fine." Then Mrs. Murphy said to me, "I'm not exactly ready to kick the bucket yet, but I'd be willing to try a wee bit of that ginger tea. Do we have any ginger root, Evelyn?"

"I believe we do," Miss Evelyn answered crisply. "You know I often steam ginger root to help you breathe easier when you get stuffed up. Truth be known, I was about to prepare a pot for you to take to your room." She gave me a sour sort of look. "I would think drinking it would not be to your liking."

"I will be the judge of that, my dear," Mrs. Murphy said. "Kami, what else do you need for the tea?"

"Honey and lemon are added to the tea after the ginger is boiled," I said, "and a dash of cinnamon."

"Evelyn?"

"Yes Mother, we have all the ingredients."

"In that case, Kami, your first assignment is to make me a pot of your grandmother's ginger tea." She coughed hard into her hankie. "It can't hurt, and I'd drink almost anything to stop this dreadful cough from ripping my chest apart."

After the tea was taken to Mrs. Murphy, Miss Evelyn said I was finished for the night, so I went into my little closet. It was warm because of its proximity to the kitchen stove. Anyway, I was so tired I could have slept in a box at a train station. I slipped into the large white nightdress that lay on the bed and slid between the stiff sheets. I don't even remember closing my eyes.

CHAPTER 11

The Accident

"MOTHER IS FEELING poorly still," Evelyn told me first thing in the morning, waking me up. "I've got a call in to the doc. 'Tis a worry, to be sure."

Reluctantly, I stuck my feet out of the warm blankets. The stove that warmed the room during the day had been cold all night, and I could almost see my breath.

"Hop to it," Miss Evelyn called from the kitchen. Then she popped her head in the doorway again. "I filled your wash pitcher. Once you've washed up, you can make breakfast."

Really? I hoped for everyone's sake, they had a toaster.

"I'm taking Mother a mustard plaster," Evelyn announced

when I appeared in the kitchen. "You'll need to poach father's eggs. He's a man of routine, that he is, and he'll be looking for his eggs shortly."

I stared at the wood stove, wondering if it would be possible to figure it out on my own.

Evelyn noticed my hesitation. "Surely you know how to poach a couple of eggs?"

"I'm not familiar with this type of stove," I said, hoping to avoid this and any future cooking assignments.

Evelyn rubbed her temples with her fingers. "Where does Mother find girls like you who can't cook a simple egg?"

I should have known it would take more than a little domestic ignorance to deter Evelyn from her task of turning me into a maid, and the lesson on the wood stove began immediately.

Lighting the wood stove, then poaching eggs in the little metal dishes turned out to be less overwhelming than I thought it would be. After the Reverend had eaten his breakfast, Evelyn let me eat one of the poached eggs with a piece of toast. The toaster was something else. That was another bit of new non-technology. It was this sad-looking wire contraption that sat on the stove. You had to lean the pieces of bread against the wire racks until they turned brown. I had always wanted to go camping, and this, I decided, was probably what it was like.

The second I swallowed the last bite of my egg, Evelyn was ready with the next assignment.

"I need you to go to Cowell's Drugs and get some medicine the moment it opens. By the time you've set the kitchen to rights, you can be on your way." Miss Evelyn took out a pad of paper and a pencil from a drawer and began to jot down the necessary information.

The weather was more vicious today than ever, and I wasn't looking forward to the walk. "Is the drugstore far?"

"Oh no. Just a hop, skip and a jump from here, on Whyte Avenue, at 105th Street. You can't miss it." Evelyn handed me two quarters. "Give the note to Mr. Cowell. He'll get the right stuff for you."

"Is this enough?" I asked, holding out the quarters.

"I should say so," Evelyn answered, then she disappeared up the stairs to check on her mother.

The note and the coins bounced against each other in my mitten as I braced myself for the swirling snow. The bitter wind stung my face, and the snow was so deep I had to walk down the middle of the road, keeping to the tracks that a lone car had made.

At 109th Street, I turned south and continued the four blocks to Whyte. From there I could see the Cowell's Drugs sign swinging wildly above the frozen awning a few blocks ahead.

A bell rang as I pushed open the door and stepped into the warmth of the store. Gleaming wood shelves were filled with jars and bottles. Wow. This was no Shopper's Drug Mart. Glass-display cases with fancy hairbrush sets, fountain pens, little silver make-up containers and all sorts of unusual trinket boxes and things sat in the middle where you couldn't miss them. At the very back of the store, there was a window where I assumed the pharmacist would be. A thin, wiry man with round gold-rim glasses met me at the window. "Mr. Cowell?" I asked, handing him the note from Miss Evelyn.

"That's me," he said, as he read the note. "It's most likely that terrible influenza bug. It's a doozy. I've heard of several cases just this week. It's none too pleasant, I can tell you that." He came out of the back room and went to a row of bottles along the far wall.

"This Kimball Cough Medicine will do the trick," he said, climbing on the stepstool to reach a bottle with a red and white label off the top shelf.

"White Pine and Tar Cough Syrup" the label said. It sounded awful. Out of habit, I checked the ingredients. "Chloroform and alcohol?" I read out loud. "Isn't chloroform what they use to knock you out before an operation?"

Mr. Cowell peered over the top of his glasses. "I'm certain there's not enough in it to knock anyone out. It calms the cough. That's the point."

"Yes, of course," I answered, thinking this stuff was probably poison. "How much does it cost?"

"Thirty cents, even."

"That's all? Wow."

Mr. Cowell laughed as I handed him the two quarters and tucked the bottle of cough medicine into my coat pocket.

"It's miserable weather out there," he said. "You tell Miss Murphy she's lucky to have a domestic to run her errands in this weather." He handed me the change.

It was friendly chatter, not intended to be mean, but still, it felt degrading to be called a "domestic." I sighed. The worst part was that it was true. I opened the door and stepped onto the sidewalk.

"Look out!" a voice yelled. I looked up to see a black motor car careening out of control, heading straight toward me. It swerved like crazy toward the sidewalk so I ran back into the store. Mr. Cowell looked up from where he was shelving stuff, but before I could say anything, there was an explosive crash of metal and glass. The Tin Lizzie had come right through the drugstore window.

As I looked inside the wrecked car, I could see that the driver's head was matted in blood and her face was a river of red. "Call an ambulance," I yelled. That's when I recognized the muskrat. Why was Mrs. Mitchell driving Lizzie?

She didn't scream or even cry. In fact, she didn't move at all.

"Good heavens, what happened?" Mr. Cowell looked horrified.

"It's Mrs. Mitchell. She's bleeding badly." I was already trying to pry open the driver's-side door but it was badly dented and refused to budge. I unwound the scarf from around my neck, reached through the window and pressed the scarf into the gash in her head, keeping as much pressure on as possible to stop the bleeding.

"I'll call emergency!" Mr. Cowell ran to the back.

A man in a dress coat rushed in. "Is anyone hurt? I heard the crash from next door." He looked at Mrs. Mitchell, limp in the driver's seat. "Good Lord."

"Get some ice," I yelled. "I'm trying to stop the bleeding but I need ice. Mr. Cowell is phoning the ambulance."

The man hesitated and I was just about to tell him to get some from outside when Mr. Cowell called from the back. "I have ice here, but the phone lines are down. I can't reach any-one."

The pharmacist came running from the back with an ice pack made from damp towels wrapped around a chunk of ice. I removed the scarf and applied the ice pack while Mr. Cowell checked her pulse. "Have you got a motor car?" he asked the man in the dress coat. "We need to get this woman to the hospital."

"No, but I'll see if I can flag a taxi cab." He ran out the door to the street.

"I don't think we should move her. We have to get help."

"I'll take over there for you," Mr. Cowell offered, stepping in to tend to Mrs. Mitchell.

"How far is the hospital?" I asked.

"The nearest one is the university hospital. It's just on the other side of the university campus."

"I'm going to run to the hospital to get help. If that man comes back with a cab, they can pick me up and take me to the hospital. We should let the medics transport her."

"The hospital may not have vehicles that can travel through

this snow. Run to the fire hall. They'll be able to help." He pointed out the window. "It's just down the street. Corner of 103rd and 83rd. You can't miss it."

Thank goodness it wasn't far. Even so, my lungs were burning from the cold by the time I reached the brick fire hall. I could barely suck in enough air to talk. "A car accident," I told the first person I saw. "A bad one. Cowell's Drugstore on Whyte Ave."

In a matter of seconds, the bell on the fire truck was clanging, the smaller ambulance vehicle travelling in its wake.

There was nothing more I could do, so I headed back to the Murphy house with the cough medicine. Miss Evelyn, no doubt, would be wondering what had happened to me.

CHAPTER 12

The "Talk"

THE MORNING AFTER the accident began the same as yesterday morning. Poached eggs for the Reverend. Miss Evelyn lit the stove for me, but I did a pretty decent job of the eggs. Because it was Sunday, Miss Evelyn buzzed about polishing the Reverend's Sunday shoes and taking the lint brush to his suit jacket. I was not disappointed to learn that I would stay behind. Miss Evelyn said I would be needed as a nursemaid to Mrs. Murphy, but I secretly thought she didn't want to show me off in public.

"Mrs. Murphy has a bell on her nightstand," Miss Evelyn told me. "If the bell rings, move smartly to see what she needs."

I was looking forward to a couple of hours away from Evelyn and her eagle eyes scrutinizing my every move, and really hoped the little bell would not ring.

No such luck. The minute the door closed behind Miss Evelyn and the Reverend, the bell jingled. Of course I ran up the stairs but stopped when I reached the closed door. This was awkward. I mean, this wasn't a sick child. This was the great Emily Murphy. The bell rang again. I stood as tall as possible and managed to plant a smile on my face. I learned that from my mother. If you're nervous, the best thing to do is to smile. It makes you look confident. Or so I hoped. Then I opened the door.

"Good morning, Kami, how did you sleep?" Mrs. Murphy said in a croaky voice.

"Good," I answered politely.

"Pull up that chair over there and humour an old lady for a bit, will you?"

I took the chair from the vanity table and put it closer to the bed. I was really hoping she only wanted a glass of water.

"On Sundays, you'll have the afternoon to do as you like. Did Miss Evelyn tell you that?"

"She did, but she's been very worried about you so I thought perhaps I would be needed this afternoon," I answered.

"Ach. My voice is a little weak. I'll be fine. Evelyn is a fusspot, but she takes good care of me, so I shouldn't complain."

Mrs. Murphy took a drink of water and lay back on her pillows for a moment. I shifted uneasily on the chair.

"Does it bother you to be a domestic servant?"

The question caught me completely off-guard. "It isn't what I would choose," I answered carefully. "But I'm very grateful that you took me in."

"You are a clever lass, Kami. I heard about how you jumped in with both feet to help Mrs. Mitchell yesterday. She is lucky you were there, and that you are a forgiving sort, after the way she tossed you aside."

"I did what anyone would have done," I answered. "If that had been my mother, I would have expected someone to act as quickly."

"Indeed." Mrs. Murphy looked thoughtful. "Unfortunately, cleverness is not likely to be your friend."

"Excuse me?"

"I sense that being a maid is distasteful to you, as though you consider yourself above that station." She paused. "You mentioned that your father is Scottish."

"His parents came from Scotland," I answered, wondering what that had to do with anything.

"Ah. Well, I can see some Scottish traits shining through, to be sure. But you are not Scottish. Not as far as society is concerned. You will always be considered Oriental. Working as a domestic, or something akin to it, is what will be available to you. Do you understand that?"

"No, I don't understand. I believe in equality. I thought you did, too."

"Kami, people arrive daily from other countries, wanting to make Canada their home. I don't blame them. It is a good country. But the fact remains that Canada is founded on British values, and those coming to our country must adhere to those British values." She began to cough, and I handed her the glass of water from her night table.

"Do British values exclude people who are Japanese?"

"Some races are known to have certain issues, shall we say, that are not in the best interest of society."

I opened my mouth to object to such a broad generalization but she held up her hand to stop me. "I'm telling you this for your own good, child. People can be rigid about such things, and it will not go well for you if you question the authority of your employer. It may be harmful to you if you try to rise above your station."

"I understand," I said, feeling more disappointed than anything. This wasn't what I expected from Emily Murphy. "May I say something?"

"When it is only the two of us, you may speak your mind. You are a puzzle, and I find you intriguing."

"One day, Canada will be considered a mosaic of many cultures and many colours. No one will care what shape my eyes are. When that day comes, I won't have to be a domestic servant."

Mrs. Murphy cocked her head to the side and smiled. "You're a dreamer, Kami. I like that. As Mr. Mitchell says, you have spunk." She paused. "It takes people of vision to cause change and you have that. But change does not come easily, my dear. I fear you have a difficult road ahead." Then she closed her eyes, and I left quietly so as not to disturb her.

After the noon meal, I finished the dishes, thinking about how I would spend my free afternoon. I was working on a plan to walk over to Helen's. Now that I had helped Mrs. Mitchell, perhaps she would be willing to let me in. I was hoping to get another look at that journal. That had to be the key to getting back home.

A loud knock at the door startled me out of my musings. When I opened the door, Helen and her father were standing there, as though my mind had conjured them up. Helen wore a grin as wide as Jasper Avenue.

"Kami, just the person we want to see," Mr. Mitchell said, a twinkle in his eyes. "We brought your clothes over in case you need them."

I stared, hardly believing my eyes. "Thanks," I said taking the bag from him. I peered inside. My jeans and my hoodie lay neatly folded in the bottom of the bag. "I didn't think I would ever see these again."

Helen beamed. "I knew you'd be happy to get your special kangaroo jacket back, although I'd love to keep it."

"Who is at the door?" Miss Evelyn came out of the kitchen, whipping off her apron as she approached the door.

"It's Mr. Mitchell and Helen," I said.

"Mr. Cowell can't say enough good things about how this young lady took charge of the situation yesterday with Millie," Mr. Mitchell told Evelyn. "She's a real heroine. Imagine, taking the initiative to run for help. I'm surprised her toes didn't fall off from the cold. The medics were impressed, too. Said she saved Mrs. Mitchell's life."

"I did hear some of the details," Miss Evelyn said. "Mr. Cowell called Mother to let her know. We're very proud of Kami." It was funny to see how she puffed up with pride at Mr. Mitchell's words, as though she were the one responsible for my actions.

"Mrs. Mitchell is resting in the hospital now," Mr. Mitchell continued. "She's going to be just fine. We want you to know, Kami, how grateful we all are, for your level-headed thinking and quick action. The doctor at the hospital said she was very lucky that someone stopped the bleeding so quickly."

I blushed at the kind words.

"Can you come to the airfield with us?" Helen blurted enthusiastically. "We're going to welcome home the pilots."

"But I thought your car was wrecked," I said.

"Lizzie is in rough shape, all right," Mr. Mitchell confirmed. "She'll be out of commission for a while. My brother, Helen's Uncle Howard, is taking us to the airfield in his motor car. He's waiting out front for us. There's no way we'd miss this event."

"Please say yes, Kami. I've missed you so much."

"That's right," Mr. Mitchell agreed. "We insist." Then he looked at Evelyn. "If it's all right with you, that is, Miss Murphy."

Miss Evelyn smiled, making her look quite pleasant. "You can tell us all about it when you return."

CHAPTER 13

The Homecoming

SIRENS SCREAMED THROUGH the streets, and motorists blasted their horns. Cars lined Portage Avenue like an endless parade of black beetles as all of Edmonton, or so it seemed, flocked to Blatchford Field.

Helen and I hopped from one foot to the other to keep warm while we watched the sky for the first sign of the pilots. It was a funny sight, everyone pointing their chins in the air, as though Chicken Little had just announced the sky was falling. People continued to pour onto the field over the next half hour. Everyone had come out to welcome the heroes home.

"Lift those banners high, kids," Mr. Mitchell shouted. I helped Helen hold up her WOP MAY SAVES THE DAY poster she had made in school, as her father snapped a picture with the world's largest camera. "The pilots should be breaking through the clouds any time now."

Everyone waved flags and hoisted their banners. Kids shook jars of rocks they had brought for noisemakers. It was crazy.

"I heard Mother talking to Mrs. Murphy on the phone before the accident," Helen said quietly so no one else could hear. "They were talking about you."

"Really? What were they saying?"

"From what I could figure out, Mrs. Murphy thinks something has snapped in your brain, causing you to behave the way you do. She thinks you might have amnesia and can't remember where you live. Mother agrees that you have some kind of mental illness."

"That's not good. I wish I could explain what's going on." Helen had spoiled the moment by telling me this. What was I supposed to do?

"She's going to have you assessed, Kami, to determine if you should be locked up."

"Locked up? In an institution?"

"The insane asylum in Ponoka, Kami. They think you might need to be committed."

"What?" I yelled. Everyone looked at me.

"Look," Helen said excitedly, pointing to the clouds. Shouts exploded from the crowd. "There they are!"

Sirens wailed and horns sounded. Sure enough, the tiny Avian broke through the clouds. Lower and lower it descended, its double wings hovering over the crowd. The plane had barely touched down when a mob burst onto the field. Mr. Mitchell's tripod and camera got knocked over as people pushed past us and onto the runway. It was amazing no one was hurt.

The plane rolled to a stop and the pilots were hoisted high as the crowd chanted their names. It was a powerful moment. The ice-covered pilots, lips bleeding, faces raw, told a story no radio broadcaster could convey.

"You can tell the world it was a cold trip," Wop May said to the crowd, trying to smile. The heroes were carried into the warm hanger to thaw as hundreds of people pushed through the doors right behind them. Because of Mr. Mitchell's press pass we were allowed in. The room filled in no time, and lots of people were turned away.

"That's the mayor of Edmonton," Helen told me, pointing to the man in the overcoat with a fur collar on the makeshift stage trying to get the crowd's attention. He started his speech over three times before the crowd settled enough for him to be heard. Even then, the crowd erupted into excited chants, so he ended with saying there would be a special ceremony on Monday for the heroic pilots, then he opened the floor to questions from the reporters.

"Captain May, we heard you had a fire on the plane at one point. Can you tell us about that?"

I felt sorry for Captain May. His lips were raw and bleeding, and he winced as he began to speak. "Someone told me that a silk scarf would prevent my lips from freezing," he began, "but the good lady neglected to mention that my skin would come off with it, so, I'll let Vic do most of the talking."

"We had a couple of close calls," his pal Vic continued. "When we landed at Stinking Lake we discovered that some garbage got a little too close to the burners and was smouldering. The second time, Wop was riding in the back and I guess his feet got a little hotter than expected. It turned out that one of the coals flipped out of the charcoal burner and a blanket covering the medicine had caught on fire."

"It was a mighty strange feeling to be freezing and burning at the same time," Wop added. Everyone laughed and then his partner continued.

"We're grateful to be home safely. And most importantly, the medicine was delivered on time, before the illness spread."

"And to the young lady who gave us those chewy bars, if you're here, we owe you a big thank you," Captain May said. "I've never tasted a bar like that before, but I can tell you, it was just the boost we needed."

"Hey, wasn't that you?" Helen nudged me with her elbow.

"Yeah, I'm glad I remembered they were in my pocket." Captain May's words warmed me. Playing even a small part in the Mission of Mercy was something I'd never forget.

After a few more questions, the heroes were ushered out the door into the waiting vehicles, and driven to their homes. The mood of the crowd was still celebratory when we piled back into Helen's uncle's car. It was a newer vehicle, with real glass windows. Horns honked and people shouted all the way through the city.

"I hope all those Edmontonians who voted against a proper airport feel like the idiots they are," Mr. Mitchell said to his brother. "Look what those men were willing to go through, and not a respectable airport or a closed-in plane available. For all those narrow-minded ninnies, it was obvious today that flying is here to stay."

I let the conversation flow over me. It was an exciting day, but my mind was on the conversation that Helen had over-heard. If she was right, I was more at risk than I had realized.

CHAPTER 14

The Plan

THE CAR STOPPED IN front of the Murphy home. I hopped out and waved to Helen. When the vehicle rounded the corner, out of sight, I glanced at the window to see if Miss Evelyn was watching. As far as I could tell, no one was looking out any of the windows, so I continued walking, casually, as though I was out for a Sunday afternoon stroll. As soon as I knew for sure I was out of sight of the Murphy house, I broke into a run and didn't stop until I reached the library.

In my desperation, I had decided that it would be better to go to the library in hopes of getting home. That was, after all, where I was when the time shifted on me again. After what

Helen said, I thought I had better try something. From what I could tell, I didn't have anything to lose.

Taking the library steps two at a time, I sprinted to the top and pulled on the heavy door. It didn't budge. That's when I saw the sign. SUNDAY — CLOSED. You've got to be kidding. For a moment, I stood there, as though waiting for the door to magically open. Then I trudged down the road, back to the Murphy house, feeling more homesick and scared than ever, if that was possible.

∽

Monday morning Evelyn cheerfully announced at 6 a.m. that it was laundry day. My eyes, puffy from lack of sleep and crying into my pillow, were not interested in opening. And, I was pretty sure, they had never seen 6 a.m. Even once I got my eyes to open, it was obvious this was not my best time of day. My fuzzy brain refused to process even the simplest task such as putting the bread on the wire toaster thingy.

I didn't fully grasp the meaning of laundry day, until I was leaning over steamy water, pulling sheets through the wringer of the Murphys' washing machine. After an hour, my back ached and my fingers were raw from the scalding water, but Miss Evelyn was so proud of their new electric washer that I didn't dare complain. At least I managed to keep my limbs intact as I fed the boiled sheets through the rollers that squeezed out the excess water. According to Miss Evelyn, this was not always the case. In between sorting the laundry and loading it into a basket to hang on the line outside, she told tales of unfortunate housewives and children who caught various body parts in the vicious wringer contraption.

When Miss Evelyn announced that it was time for us to take our tea, I suddenly realized that it was after ten. The library would be open now. My plan was to go out for a walk during my break and then take a detour to the library. I hadn't realized that Miss Evelyn and I would have "tea" together.

"You make Mother more of your medicinal ginger tea," Miss Evelyn instructed, "and I'll make us some devilled eggs with ham."

Tea, I was beginning to realize, was any time there was a break and usually involved food. I peeled the ginger root and was putting the water on to boil when Miss Evelyn casually mentioned that Mrs. Bell from the Children's Aid Society was coming over later on this morning.

The pot dropped from my hand, and water hissed over the hot stove.

"Pay attention to what you're about," Miss Evelyn scolded, as she grabbed a towel to wipe up the water that was now dripping over the polished floor.

"Sorry," I mumbled.

"I didn't think that bit of news would startle you to kingdom come," she said, her narrowed eyes looking sharply in my direction. "You didn't think you were staying here, surely."

"Of course not," I said, but the news had caught me totally off-guard. I hadn't thought it would happen so fast.

"Good, because with mother not well, she doesn't need the strain of worrying about you on top of it all. And I have my hands full without extra duties."

Extra duties? Was that what I was? It was a heartless thing to say after I had worked so hard without complaining. I had allowed myself to think that Evelyn was beginning to like me.

I decided that the main thing was to not arouse any suspicion and to get out of here before they shipped me off to the Children's Aid. I turned the knob on the damper of the stove the way Evelyn had showed me. I wanted this water to boil as quickly as possible. First I would make the tea, and then I'd figure out a way to slip out the door when Evelyn wasn't looking.

"As soon as you have made the tea, you'll have to do a quick swipe of the silver. We have a lot of work yet to do and precious little time for it, but it wouldn't do to serve Mrs. Bell tea with a smudged spoon, now would it?"

Miss Evelyn brought the silver chest to the table and handed me a little tin of cream and a rag. "A dab of cream then rub, then rinse them in hot water and shine them again."

"I can do these on my own," I suggested. "You go ahead and do whatever else needs to be done." I smiled as sweetly as possible.

But Evelyn didn't leave. She hovered like a mother hen, inspecting every piece so all I could do was polish the stupid silverware.

It felt like forever, but finally Miss Evelyn disappeared for a moment and I had my chance to make a run for it. I slipped into my little room and grabbed the bag with my jeans that Helen had brought yesterday.

"These are for you," Miss Evelyn said, suddenly appearing at the doorway. In one hand was a plain brown dress and in the other some brown socks.

I swallowed hard, casually dropping the bag of clothes behind me. "They are?" Was all I managed to get out. I hadn't expected her to pop into my room like that. The dress, made from heavy canvas, was so ugly I felt sure it was designed to elicit pity from Mrs. Bell, or anyone else they could convince to take me.

"I made this up for you last night when I found out Mrs. Bell was stopping by. You need to have something else to wear."

"Thank you," I said, knowing this was the required response, even though I wasn't feeling even a tiny bit thankful.

"Hop to it. Make yourself presentable."

For one awful moment I thought she was going to stand right there waiting until I put on the horrid dress, but then she continued, "I need to get Mother ready now. Her hair will be a disaster and she'll want to look her best." She disappeared down the hall, and I heard her even, plodding steps as she mounted the stairs.

Finally I hung the dress on the nail on the wall and took my jeans and hoodie out of the paper sack. "Thank you Helen," I whispered as I put them on. My heart pounded hard against my ribs as I slipped out of the room and tiptoed to the front door. Thank goodness Mrs. Murphy's bedroom was at the back of the house.

I turned the knob slowly to avoid loud clicking noises, pulled the door open and smacked right into a woman who I could only presume was Mrs. Bell, practically knocking her over in the process.

"What in heaven's name?"

I hesitated for a second, which was a mistake.

"Where do you think you're going?" The cheerful smile was a complete contradiction to the vice-like grip the woman had on my arm. But then the adrenaline kicked in big time. It was all or nothing and I decided on *all*. I let out a murderous scream, wrenching my body free from the bewildered woman and ran as though my life depended on it.

I ran all the way to the library, flew up the front steps and burst through the door. Then I stopped and forced myself to walk calmly past the checkout desk to avoid drawing attention to myself. As I walked past the newspaper rack, the headline from the *Edmonton Journal* jumped out at me. "Most Tumultuous Welcome in History of This City for 'Wop' May and Vic Horner." That's it — the end of the story I had been reading when the centuries flip-flopped on me. My hands shook as I tried to slide the paper carefully off the rung of the paper rack. Another paper caught the edge and came off as well, falling into a mess on the floor. I nervously glanced at the front door, hoping the evil Bell lady had not followed me. I contemplated leaving the paper on the floor so that I could get out of view of the front door, but the librarian's eagle eye was now on me. I picked up the paper and draped it as quickly as possible over the top dowel.

The sign on the wall near the back of the main room read MEN'S READING ROOM, and there was an arrow pointing down the stairs. I pulled the hoodie up over my hair, hoping I could pass as a boy. Holding the newspaper article in front of my face, I headed toward the stairs. That's when I heard the shrill voice of Mrs. Bell calling out to the librarian, "Did a girl wearing dungarees come in here?"

Oh no. I began to read the article, quickly moving toward the stairwell at the same time. If this didn't work, I didn't have a Plan B.

"Ow." I ran into the corner of a table and dropped the paper.

CHAPTER 15

Drew

"ARE YOU OKAY?" a voice mumbled, followed by some throat-clearing noises.

The newspaper was nowhere in sight, but the voice belonged to a guy, probably close to my age, with dark curls springing out every which direction. For some reason he had Helen's journal in his hand.

"Where did you get that?" I asked. My brain felt like cotton fluff.

"The floor. I was going to turn it in but ..." he shrugged, "apparently I don't have to."

He handed the journal to me and I couldn't help noticing

his clothing. Baggy jeans. Snoop Dogg T-shirt. "Hey, you look normal," I blurted.

"Not the best compliment, but eh . . ." He shrugged. "I'll take it."

"No, I mean . . . Oh never mind. I can't believe I'm really here." My knees buckled and I grabbed hold of the nearest shelf to steady myself.

"Are you okay? 'Cause, I can get the library staff or something if you want."

"No, no. I'm good. Really. Just a little dizzy is all." I studied my surroundings carefully to convince myself that I was really back. There they were: the ugly, grey security gates. I had never seen anything so beautiful in all my life. "Yes!" I cheered under my breath. Then I realized that the guy was still standing in front of me, his eyebrows rising under his black curls.

"Have you ever gone anywhere so far away, you thought you'd never get home?" I asked.

"Like Mars, you mean?"

"Yeah. Exactly."

"No." He shook his head and grinned. "Drew," he offered, by way of introduction. "And you are?" He stuffed his hands into his jeans pockets.

"Kami," I said, taking in every tiny indication of the twenty-first century. It had worked. By some beautiful, amazing miracle, it worked. I had gone back to the library, and then the newspaper article was hanging right there. Maybe that was it. Maybe it was because I was reading that newspaper story. It was the same story . . .

"Let me just say," Drew's voice interrupted my meanderings, "that you are the strangest girl I have ever met. Seriously. You've made my day."

"Well then, that makes us even," I said. "Oh, not the strange part, but . . ."

He put his hand up to prevent me from embarrassing myself further. "No need to explain. I take anything not outrageously rude as a compliment, so you don't have to worry."

"All right, then. We're good." I looked at the clock on the wall. 2:50. "Hey, do you know what the date is?"

"Yup. It's October 15th."

"October 15th? This is *still* October 15th?" That did not make sense.

"Long day, I guess, eh?"

"Long. That would be one way to describe it. Well, thanks for picking up my book. I have to get going." Even though everything appeared normal, I desperately needed to get to my grandparents' house and make sure.

"I'll walk to the door with you, in case you have another dizzy spell."

"I'm fine. Really," I said, but he walked with me anyway. "Why aren't you in school, by the way?"

"This is my school," he said, pointing back to the table with a laptop on it. "I do all my courses online."

"Why?"

He shrugged. "Less walking. You know, between classes."

We had reached the door, and I was seriously hoping he wasn't planning on walking me home. "Maybe I'll see you around."

"Cool. I'm here every day if you're ever in the mood for another off-the-wall conversation."

"Good to know." Without looking back, I walked out the door into the brisk autumn air and took a deep breath. It smelled of mouldy leaves and dead grass. I couldn't get enough of it. "I love you 2004!" I yelled to the sky, and I didn't care who thought I was crazy.

When I reached the house, Mom was just driving into the driveway. Oh my gosh. Was Mom only now coming home from her meeting? That didn't seem possible.

"How was your day?" she asked as I hopped in.

"Exhausting." I closed my eyes. Thank goodness, I was home.

"Come on in and help me measure a few things." It sounded like Mom was rustling around in her purse for something.

I groaned. "Really, Mom? Can't it wait until tomorrow?"

"What did you do that was so exhausting?"

It was so long ago that it took me a minute even to re-member the beginning of the day. I looked up at the attic window. "I moved a lot of boxes. Did you know that the attic was full of boxes?"

"Why on earth would you do that, and where did you move them to? I'm almost afraid to ask."

"The attic is my new loft bedroom, and I moved them to the first bedroom at the top of the stairs."

"Good grief." Mom put the car in reverse and backed out of the driveway. "You're right. I can't deal with this tonight. Let's go to the hotel."

"Excellent," I said. "I'm dying for a hot shower."

"I thought we'd eat at the hotel tonight," Mom said. "That way I can have a glass of wine and relax without having to drive."

"Yeah, I like that idea. The not-driving part, at least. I'm not big on wine."

"Funny girl. Just a heads-up, I invited Bernie, the architect, to join us. He had some plans he wanted to show me, and I didn't want to stay at the office any longer. I knew you were waiting for me."

"What? How could you do that? This was supposed to be our time together. You're always working. Always. Even when you're not working, you're working. I might as well be an orphan." The words were out of my mouth before I realized what I had said. The overly bright smile of the Children's Aid lady flashed before my eyes.

"Lucky for you, he has a son your age he's bringing along so you won't have to sit and listen to the boring shop-talk."

"You're joking, right? Please tell me you're joking." I couldn't believe my mother had done this. "Maybe I'll skip supper altogether and go to bed."

"I'll make you a deal. We'll get through this dinner tonight. Just be cordial and listen to his brilliant son, and then tomorrow is all yours. Promise. It's Saturday, so you don't have to go to school, and I told everyone at the office that, unless there's an emergency, I'm not available. We'll hang out and eat junk food and figure out what to keep and what to pitch."

"Eat junk food?" I raised my eyebrows.

"That's what teenagers like, right?"

"Mom, your idea of junk food is white rice." I sighed, knowing I would agree to the dinner. The guilt would consume me if I didn't. "Okay, fine. But I'm having a shower first. A long hot shower, and don't be surprised if I fall asleep in my food at dinner. It's been a long day already."

"Deal. How many boxes were there, for heaven's sake?"

"You'd be amazed," I said, knowing I would never tell my mother what happened.

⚮

"So, his son is brilliant?" I said, as we stepped into the hotel elevator to go down to the restaurant.

"Relax, Kami. I'm sure he's no smarter than you. His dad is proud of him because he's fourteen and already in university."

"Oh yeah, that's just like me," I said sarcastically. "You didn't tell me his son was a geek."

"If by *geek* you mean intelligent, I guess he is," Mom said, checking her hair in the elevator mirror. "But that's hardly a fault."

I groaned. "How could you subject me to a Mensa nerd on my first day in town? My vocabulary consists of one- and two-syllable words. I won't even know what he's talking about."

"Nonsense. You're extremely articulate, Kami. You were

spelling words on your little magnet board when you were two. And anyway, it's dinner. You're not finding a cure for cancer." The door opened on the main floor. "I bet half my team were geeks when they were your age," Mom continued. "Having a functional brain when you're a teenager is not all bad, you know."

Easy for her to say. She was beautiful and brainy — a winning combination at any age. "Just promise me that you won't start talking about how I could spell at two."

"Or about when you flushed your toothpaste down the toilet so you wouldn't have to brush your teeth?"

"Mom!" Clearly, this dinner was a bad idea.

The hostess led us to a table where Mom's friend and his teen prodigy were already seated. I pretended to look at the view out the window as we approached the table, even though it was already getting dark and I couldn't see a thing.

The architect guy jumped up and pulled out the chair for Mom while I looked nowhere in particular, avoiding everyone's eyes.

"Hey, Kami. Didn't think I'd see you again so soon." A familiar voice said.

You've got to be kidding. There was Drew, sitting under his big goofy grin, beside his dad, the architect. I laughed. "This has been the weirdest day of my entire life."

"But in a good way, right?" Drew commented.

"You two know each other?" Mom said, her smile tightening into a line. "You didn't say anything about meeting anyone today." Mom bristled. She doesn't like being surprised or embarrassed, and I think she was a little of both.

"We met at the library," Drew said.

"This is Drew's father, Mr. Keegan," Mom said in her cool, too polite voice that she uses when something bugs her.

I smiled at Mr. Keegan and we shook hands. It didn't take Mom and Mr. Keegan long to get into the work jargon, which I didn't mind so much, now that Drew was the Mensa geek.

"So, you're a university student," I said. His smile faded, and I realized that it was the wrong thing to say.

"Apparently my reputation as a freak of nature has taken over once more." There was an awkward silence.

"Sorry, I guess you hear that all the time."

"No biggie. It's not your fault. I just wish my father could be a little more creative when talking about me. That's what was so great about meeting you this afternoon. You had no idea who I was and we could just talk. It was fun. Now that you've heard I have this cerebral quirk, you'll be all weird and not know what to say."

"I may not have a supersized brain, but I'm not a housefly. I think I can hold up my end of the conversation," I said, trying to sound confident.

He laughed. "Man, I'm brutal. That's one of the hazards of online learning. My social skills suck."

After that we got onto the topic of favourite things to do, which went much better. I told him that I got my red belt in Tae Kwon Do last year, and was hoping to get my first degree black belt soon. Of course, at the moment, I was without an instructor.

He loved photography and archaeology. He told me about actual digs he went on and about the fossils and gems he found. It sounded pretty cool. I also learned that his mom died of cancer a year ago, so I told him about my dad. I wasn't expecting to, but it just kind of came out.

Before I knew it, the dinner meeting was over, and it was time to go. I had to admit Drew was fun to talk to. Not at all what I expected from a fourteen-year-old university student.

CHAPTER 16

The New School

MOVING DAY WENT well, given my mother's high maintenance perfectionism. Those movers couldn't wait to get out of here. I was pretty glad it was over, too. We had been living out of our suitcases at the hotel while Mom dealt with cleaners and storage people. We had to postpone the movers twice already, and Mom had also postponed our just-the-two-of-us day until moving day. She couldn't afford to be away from work more than that. Not now. Not at the beginning of the project.

We didn't exactly have heart-to-heart talks, and Mom steered clear of any questions about my father with the skill of a Formula One race-car driver, but we did okay. We didn't even argue much about where to put our stuff and how to organize the rooms. That's why I was completely blindsided by the bomb she dropped at supper.

We were celebrating our first night in the house by having a giant plate of nachos dripping with cheese, when Mom got all fidgety. I figured she must have heard something about my father — something I didn't want to hear.

"You know, Kami," she said, finally. "I was talking to Drew's father today."

"Really?" That was kind of odd.

"He mentioned that Drew went to this amazing lady to talk about things after his mother passed away."

"By *amazing lady*, you mean psychologist, right? I'm not six, Mom. I know what a psychologist is. Did you hear from Dad? Is that what this is about?"

"It's not a bad thing, you know, going to a psychologist. It doesn't mean there is something wrong with you. It would simply give you someone to talk to about things."

"My mother hasn't passed away. I could talk to you, but you're hardly ever around. And then, when you are here, you want to talk about finding some stranger for me to talk to." It made me mad when Mom thought she could just hire solutions, as she did at work. "What do you want me to talk about, anyway?"

"I know you weren't thrilled with this move. And now that we're in Edmonton, I'm sure you'll be seeing your father. I may not be the right person to talk to about everything."

"Did he go?" I asked.

"Did *who* go where?"

"Drew. Did he go to the psychologist?"

"Of course he did, honey. That's why Bernie recommended her."

"Okay, I'll make you a deal. I'll talk to Drew and ask him how helpful he found the counselling sessions. If he says they were helpful, I'll go."

Mom beamed. "That's my girl. All I'm asking is for you to consider it."

The truth was, I only agreed because I wanted an excuse to talk to Drew on Monday, and this seemed as good a reason as any.

"The phone line is connected if you want to call Becca," Mom said, knowing that would cheer me up.

"Sure. It beats unpacking." I took the cordless phone up to the attic, happy that I actually had my bed in there now. I punched in Becca's number.

"Hey, Kami. You finally got a phone. Yay!"

"I got your email. I so wish I was there. Don't tell me anything about the soccer team."

"How's your new school?"

"I start Monday. Do you realize I won't know a single person?"

"You never have trouble making friends."

"You and I have been friends since first grade. This will be the first time ever that I won't know even one person," I whined.

"Just keep under the radar for a few days," she suggested.

"What's that supposed to mean?" Like I was planning on setting off the fire alarm on my first day.

"You know. Don't ask a bunch of questions that show you don't know what's going on. And don't answer questions either, to make it look like you're a know-it-all. Just hang-out for a few days. Get a sense of who's in, who's out. That sort of thing."

"Really?" As if I cared who was "in" and who was "out."

After that, Becca chatted away about a project she was working on with this new kid, which made me more homesick. I didn't really want to hear that she was having fun without me.

By the time I got off the phone, I was dreading my first day. How could you make new friends by just "hanging out"? Becca was an observer. Not me. I was more of a blurter. Whenever a thought flew into my conscious brain, I spewed it out without giving it a second thought. I sighed as I dug through my suitcase for something to wear. Becca was probably right. Considering my recent school experience with Helen, maybe I had better try to keep a low profile.

∞

The new school was not that scary, and I actually found my classes fairly easily. I even managed to keep my mouth shut, as Becca suggested. So far, so good. Social Studies was my final class of the day, then I'd head to the library to see Drew.

I checked the number of the room against my schedule and double-checked the name on the door, as I had with all of my classes. Ms. Williams. This was it. I walked into a room with five rows of desks.

A huge banner with the words: YES! WOMEN ARE PERSONS! OCTOBER 18, 1929 was draped across the board. Surrounding the headline were the names of the Famous Five: Emily Murphy, Nellie McClung, Irene Parlby, Louise McKinney and Henrietta Muir Edwards. Panic squeezed all the air out of my lungs. I checked my phone. October 18, 2004. Whew! The fact that this classroom still had an old blackboard instead of a white board didn't help. The kids, though, were dead giveaways. Slouching in their chairs with ripped jeans and T-shirts, they certainly did not belong in 1929.

SEVENTY-FIFTH ANNIVERSARY OF THE "PERSONS" CASE, a poster advertised. That would explain it. Still, studying the Famous Five on my first day in the new school was a little creepy.

"Why would women *not* be considered 'persons'?" Ms. Williams asked the class.

"Because they're aliens," a guy from the back row shouted out.

"Hey, good one, Ty," another added, laughing.

A blonde girl in the front row shot her hand up, so the teacher quickly moved on to her.

"Because at the time the British North America Act was written, women's work was in the home raising the children," she said. "They didn't even have the vote. So, any reference to 'persons,' referred to men, not women." The girl beamed at the teacher, who in turn was smiling.

Class clowns and teacher's pets. It was the same no matter what school you went to. At least some things were predictable.

Ms. Williams liked the teacher's pet's answer. "That's exactly what the Supreme Court of Canada had previously decided." She flashed a quote on the screen. "Women are persons in the matter of pain and penalties, but not in the matter of rights and privileges."

Ms. Williams raved on about what a victory for women the decision by the Privy Council was to reject the Supreme Court's decision, and how it opened the door for women to be leaders, specifically members of the Senate. She praised Emily Murphy for leading her band of colleagues to a successful victory in recognizing women as persons.

The teacher's enthusiasm bothered me. Now that I had seen 1929 up close, well, some of the shine had tarnished. Emily Murphy wasn't as perfect as I had envisioned. Everyone in 1929, including Mrs. Murphy, was pretty racist. She thought I could be nothing more than a domestic servant. The whole thing made me sad. As a heroine, Emily Murphy had slipped from celebrity to something much more human. It made me wonder if other heroes I admired were equally flawed. I put my hand in the air.

"Yes, um . . ." Ms. Williams looked down her list for my name.

"Kami," I said. "I just moved here from Vancouver."

"Why?" Someone yelled from the back and everyone laughed, reminding me that I had failed the "keep under the radar" plan.

"You had a question, Kami?"

"Not exactly a question. I just wanted to say that even though the Famous Five gained ground for some women, society at that time was not big on equality. I mean, it wasn't only women who struggled with the issue of rights."

"Go on. Explain what you mean."

"Well, for example, today when I came to school, no one stared at me because I'm part Japanese. In 1929, if you were an Asian teen you could look forward only to being a maid to a British household. And you wouldn't be welcome at the local school." Gosh you'd think I was on a lecture tour. I stopped talking and sank low into my chair.

"Sounds like you were there," one of the goofs from the back commented.

"Maybe I was," I shot back. More laughter. Obviously I wasn't capable of "keeping under the radar." Note to self: Keep your mouth shut.

"Settle down everyone." Ms. Williams' voice rose above the laughter. "Kami brings up an interesting point. What rights, or I should say *whose* rights, were the Famous Five fighting for? Recently there has been some discussion that fits exactly with what Kami is saying. Critics today suggest Emily Murphy was racist. In her book *The Black Candle*, she blames the drug problem on the Chinese. Was she racist? If so, does that change her status as a hero?" Ms. Williams paused. You could practically see her brain picking up speed. Then her eyes grew bright, a sign I would soon recognize to mean a large assignment was about to spew forth, like hot lava.

"Kami. What a great idea you have given me."

What? What idea? This couldn't be good.

"This topic would be ideal for a debate, which is exactly what each of you will prepare for," she continued, the words building up momentum. "You will choose one of the Famous Five women to study in detail. In two week's time, you will come to class prepared to give your opinion as to whether or not your subject has earned the status to become a true heroine."

Thankfully, the bell rang to put me out of my misery. So much for making any friends in this class. I packed up my books, anxious to exit the building.

At least the first day was over, and now I could visit Drew at the library. I really wanted to tell him about the whole journal thing but wasn't sure if I had the nerve. I stopped for a washroom break and to brush my hair. Not that I needed to impress him, but I didn't want to look like something the cat dragged in either.

The washroom was empty, but as I closed the door on the first stall, giggly voices entered.

"What a loser," one of the voices sneered.

"Did you hear how she spouted off about Emily Murphy as if she was some kind of expert?"

I covered my mouth to prevent the gasp from escaping.

"I know, I mean she practically begged Williams to give us that ridiculous homework assignment. A debate? How stupid is that?"

Peeking through the crack I saw that one of the girls was blond with purple stripes in her hair and the other had long black hair, cut in sharp triangle-like points at the bottom. Careful not to move a muscle or even breathe, I hoped they weren't going to wait for this stall. The blond girl put on some bright red lip gloss and fluffed the purple strands with her fingers.

"Hey, wanna teach Know-It-All-New-Girl a lesson?"

"Ooh, sounds devious. Got a plan?" Triangle Hair responded.

"I say we make life around here a little icy for the I-Just-Moved-Here-From-Vancouver princess," Purple Stripes said.

"As in, spread the word and she'll be wondering why she can't make any friends?"

"Precisely. You talk to Vanessa and Carmen and tell them to pass it on. I'll tell Sophie and Crystal."

"I haven't had this much fun since we made those mysterious phone calls to that Goldi-loser in seventh grade." Then the two giggled their way out of the washroom.

I waited until I was sure they weren't going to come back, then I came out of the stall, still shaking. There was no way I was taking the city bus home today. I was afraid I'd meet kids from that horrible Socials class. Did everyone think the same as those girls?

It took thirty minutes to walk to the library, but I didn't care. I was just glad that I didn't see any of the kids from school. When I walked past the check-out desk at the library, I spotted Drew at the back table hunkered over his computer.

"You didn't tell me you were the daughter of famous urban designer, Keiko Kishida," Drew said when I sat down.

"If I'd known you were going to be so impressed, I'm sure it's the first thing I would have mentioned."

"No sarcasm there."

"Working on a big assignment?" I gestured to the stack of books piled higher than his computer screen.

He nodded. "That's all my father has talked about for the past two weeks."

"Your assignment?"

"Your mother."

"Yeah, she has that effect on people."

"Hey, how was your first day of school?"

"I'm thinking of joining the online crowd."

"Ouch. That doesn't sound good."

"It was okay."

"You're a terrible liar."

"You don't even know me."

"And yet, I already know you're a terrible liar."

"Okay, let's just say the friendliness factor was a little underwhelming."

"As in the girls were mean to you."

"A little. How did you know?"

"New girl. Good-looking. Confident. Think about it,

Kami. You didn't seriously think they'd be handing out BFF buttons did you?"

I blushed. "I had friends in my old school."

"You'll have friends. Give it time." Drew grinned. "I bet the guys were happy to see you."

"Enough already. Anyway, I didn't come here to talk about my first day of school."

He feigned a hurt look. "You mean you didn't come in to ask my opinion on social culture in the local school? I'm crushed."

"Actually, I did want to ask your opinion about something."

He leaned back in his chair and stretched his legs out. "Now we're talking. Go ahead. Ask Dr. Drew."

"So, Dr. Drew, is it true that when you don't have all the answers you see a therapist?" I meant it to sound funny but from the look on his face I could tell he didn't find it amusing. "Seriously, my mother thinks that because my dad disappeared and stuff that I should see a psychologist," I chattered, trying to erase the awkward moment. "Your dad told my mother that you saw this really great person and that maybe I should see her." I paused, hoping he wasn't too mad at me. "I promised that I would ask your opinion," I finished lamely.

"I knew it. I knew no good would come from those two seeing each other."

To my relief, he actually laughed. But then his words sunk in. "Seeing each other? You make it sound as though there's something going on between them. They work together, that's all."

Drew's sceptical face suggested I had just crawled out of a hole. "Seriously?"

"My mother's too busy. She never has time for anything but work."

"And that's why they talk on the phone every night and meet for drinks after work? I know a workaholic when I see one. But the way Dad twitches if I'm talking to him when the phone rings has nothing to do with architecture, trust me."

I flipped open my phone and pretended to check the time. "The movers came Saturday and I still have a ton of unpacking to do. And homework. Lots of homework."

"I'm sure she was fine," Drew said.

"What?"

"As psychologists go, I'm sure she was fine," Drew continued. "Not that I needed one."

"So, why did you go?" I asked, glad to get off the topic of my mother.

"The path of least resistance."

"Meaning?"

"Meaning that if I didn't go, I would have to endure months of badgering about the benefits I was missing out on, and then there would be the discussions as to why I wouldn't go, etc., etc. Instead, I see the nice psychologist lady, tell her everything she wants to hear, tell my dad everything he wants to hear, and before you know it, I'm a well-balanced individual. Everyone is happy."

"Hmm." Not a bad strategy actually, but I really didn't care about the dumb psychologist. Drew's comments about my mom and his dad really bugged me. Everything was going wrong, and having some lame counsellor tell me *life sucks, work with it,* was not going to help. The library suddenly felt hot and stuffy. "Well, gotta' go."

"Sure." Was there a little disappointment in his voice? "I'll be here tomorrow if you change your mind."

"If I change my mind about what?"

"What's really bugging you."

"So, you're the psychologist now?" I snapped.

"Sorry you had a rough day, Kami." He turned back to his computer and began to type.

I hesitated a second and then walked away. *Wonderful.* I made enemies my first day at school and then shot down the one person who might have been a friend. Those girls at school were right. I am a loser.

CHAPTER 17

A Risky Decision

"HOW'S THE NEW SCHOOL?" Mom asked as she chopped vegetables for the salad.

"Today is the 75th anniversary of the 'Women as Persons' case, which gave the teacher the brilliant idea about assigning a debate." I knew better than to mention that it had anything to do with racism or that I prompted the discussion.

Nevertheless, she jumped right in. "When is the anniversary of the day the Japanese in Canada got the vote? Is that taught in schools?" Mom whacked the red onion with extra force.

Here we go.

"Here's the thing about the 'Persons' case," Mom said, waving the knife in the air. "The Japanese people were not *persons* for almost two decades *after* British women became *persons*. I hope you'll include that in your debate."

"Maybe I'll just finish making the salad," I said, taking the knife from her hand.

"The Canadian Citizen Act took effect in 1947 and the Japanese got the vote in 1948," Mom continued. "I find it disturbing that there is such hype about women getting the vote in 1916, and women becoming persons in 1929, when lots of people born in Canada didn't have voting power for years. We became a country in 1867, Kami. Eighty years before allowing all Canadians the right to vote."

Whew. Did that ever hit a nerve. "On another topic, how was work?" I asked. One thing I did not need was my mother getting involved in my debate assignment.

"Busy, busy. But I have a good team and things are starting to come together."

"Speaking of your talented team, are you going out with Bernie?" I blurted. There. I said it.

Mom didn't make eye contact, and her cheeks took on a pinkish glow. "Oh my gosh, it *is* true. I can't believe it. My mother is dating an architect from work, and I had to find out from the architect's son." Mom and I didn't have the girl-friend-type of relationship, like Becca and her mom, but you'd think she'd at least confide in me if there was someone else in her life. I thought back to the dinner the other night. Everyone knew but me. I was such an idiot.

"Kami, it's not like we're dating or anything, if that's what you're thinking."

"Well, what is it like, Mom? 'Cause Drew thinks it's like dating."

"We're friends, Kami. That's what it's like. It's like having a friend. We talk on the phone and sometimes we go for coffee after work to wind down a bit before hitting the traffic. I didn't realize I needed to check with you first."

"It just bugs me that you want me to talk to this psychologist lady, and you don't even talk to me."

"I guess you failed to notice that I came home early today because I want to hear all about my daughter's first day of school."

"You're home early. So what. Do you want a medal?"

The warmth drained from my mother's face, but I kept going, like a pot boiling over. "Do you want to hear about my day? Fine. I'll tell you about school. I hate it. I hate the teachers and I hate the kids. I should never have left Vancouver. It's all your fault. How could you ruin my life? Everything always works out for you. You have a high-power job and new friends and I have nothing." I pushed my chair back forcefully, knocking it over in the process. "And some dumb psychologist can't fix it."

I ran out of the kitchen and up to my attic room. What a mess. What a ridiculous, horrible mess this whole move was.

A few minutes later there was a soft knock at the door, which I chose to ignore. Mom came in anyway. "I'm sorry your first day at school did not go as well as you had hoped, but there are a couple of things that we need to clear up before you decide what you're going to do next."

What *I* was going to do? What was she talking about? Reluctantly, I turned to face her.

"First, do not ever disrespect your mother like that again, if you hope to have the use of a cell phone or a computer in this lifetime. Second, as your parent, it is my responsibility to make certain decisions that I feel are best. How you respond to those decisions, however, is entirely up to you." Mom paused for a moment. "I do work hard to have a successful career. But I have been equally diligent in making time to attend all of your special functions and games. And that is not always easy."

"I'm sorry," I mumbled. It was true. Even with her busy schedule, she rarely missed my martial arts competitions or my soccer games. Mom wasn't big on public shows of emotion, but I always knew she cared. "You don't happen to have a couple of plane tickets for Vancouver do you?"

"No. No plane tickets. But I do have something that may be of interest to you."

"Really? What?"

"Come down and have some of your favourite perogies and I'll show you."

Curiosity got the best of me. That and hunger pangs. I was suddenly starving. When I entered the kitchen, Mom was putting the steaming perogies into a bowl on the table. Beside my plate was an ornately carved wooden box.

"What's this?" I asked, picking up the decorative box that smelled like cedar.

"I've been keeping some papers of your family history until you were old enough to appreciate them. When we were packing to move, I found this box in the bottom of my filing cabinet. Perhaps now that you are studying Canadian history, it would be a good time for you to have a look at your own history."

I opened the box. There were several newspaper clippings. Some of them were really old. "These are all people I'm related to?" I asked, leafing through them.

"Your ancestors have made great contributions to this country. You should be very proud of your heritage."

I picked up a poor quality photo of a man in front of a Japanese garden. "Wow. This one is from almost a hundred years ago. I didn't know you had these."

Mom looked over my shoulder. "Isaburo Kishida was my great grandfather. He came over from Japan to help his son build Victoria's first Japanese Tea Garden."

I put the clipping back in the box. "Thanks, Mom. I'll look at these later."

"I'm surprised you don't remember Jiichan talking about that when we visited the Gardens a couple of summers ago."

"Sometimes Jiichan tells every detail about things and I kind of tune out."

"The Kishidas are leaders and trailblazers. We stand on our own two feet. Some day you will follow in your ancestors' footsteps and make your own amazing contribution."

No pressure there. I hoped Mom was not seriously thinking I could include any of this stuff in my "Women as Persons" research. I picked up the box and moved it out of the
way. Under the box was a white envelope. "More family history?" I asked, picking it up.

"Yes, but that is from your father's side of the family. It's all
I have, so you may as well have that, too."

"Really?" I tried not to let on how excited I was as I fumbled with the envelope. Inside was a yellowed piece of paper
with ratty edges. It appeared to be a family tree. "Is this Dad's
family?" I scanned the names, quickly coming to my father's
name. But it was another name that jumped off the paper at
me. "Helen Mitchell?" I gasped. "Helen Mitchell is Dad's
grandmother?"

"Your great-grandmother. That's right." Mom's eyes narrowed. "You couldn't possibly remember her. You were only
little the last time you saw her."

"I remember she had the most beautiful blue eyes I have
ever seen." Helen was my great-grandmother. Imagine that.
Helen was my great-grandmother.

"Interesting," Mom said, giving me a strange look.

All through supper and for the rest of the evening I
couldn't stop thinking about Helen. It made sense that Dad
had kept his grandmother's journal, but now I had more
questions than ever.

After I fell asleep, my mind continued to conjure up bits

and pieces of everything that had happened, weaving them into a crazy dream that made no sense. I woke up in a sweat about something that had gone wrong, but I couldn't remember what it was. All I could remember was Helen calling me to come back. It felt so real, as though she were reaching through the years to talk to me.

I didn't think I'd be able to sleep now, so I pulled on my robe and tip-toed down the stairs trying to keep to the edges where the squeaks weren't as loud. When I reached the kitchen, I poured myself some milk and heated it in the microwave. Then I sat at the kitchen table, in the same spot where Helen and I sat drinking our cocoa.

If only I had known she was my great-grandmother at the time. I would have said something more meaningful, something she could remember over the years. I would have made more of an effort to see her again and stick some little keepsake of hers in my pocket to bring back. I would have said a proper goodbye. If only.

A tiny seed of an idea began to form. Should I go back to 1929 one more time? It was a crazy idea. What difference would it make, really? And, what ingenious words would I say? *Did you know that I'm your great-granddaughter?* She thought I was crazy as it was. I already had her journal as a keepsake. Well, sort of. It wasn't technically mine. Yeah, there was no rational reason to risk going back to 1929 again. What if I got stuck there?

I finished my hot milk and tiptoed back upstairs. Going

back to 1929 involved too many risks. Look at how long I had been there the last time without knowing how to get home. Of course no time had passed in this century, so no one had missed me. I crawled under the covers and closed my eyes. But sleep didn't come. Did Helen wonder what happened to me? Did she think I didn't care? She had been a good friend. It wasn't really how you treated a good friend.

I punched up my pillow to make it puffier and turned on my other side. If Helen understood the risk I had to take, of course she wouldn't expect me to come back just to say good-bye. No one would. My hands shook as I pulled the journal out from its hiding place under the mattress. I opened it and then quickly snapped it closed, but I didn't put it back. I had to look at Helen's face one more time, knowing she was my great-grandmother. It was like a magnetic pull that I couldn't resist. I had to go.

Still clutching the journal in my hands, I closed my eyes. Okay, I needed to think this through. For one thing, I was wearing pyjamas. Not a good idea. Arriving in winter — also not a good idea. This time of year would be good. My eyes popped open. Emily Murphy won the Persons Case on October 18 in 1929. That was it. I bet Helen included a newspaper article about that. Before I checked to find out, though, I needed to find something to wear. Something less conspicuous than jeans and my striped runners. My black Mary-Jane shoes would work better, but I definitely didn't have any sailor blouses or navy skirts. In the corner of the room was a box of clothes I hadn't unpacked yet. I began to rifle through it. Did I own a dress? Let's see. Ah ha. There it was, at the very bottom, a green velvet dress that Mom had bought for my cousin's wedding last Christmas. A little fancy, but at least it wasn't denim or sparkly. And it was classy — not something the daughter of a laundry lady would wear. Perfect.

I put on the velvet dress, did up the straps on my black shoes and brushed my hair into a coppery sheen. It was strange, but the outfit gave me confidence. I felt more in control. At that moment nothing seemed impossible.

My wool dress coat was in the front-hall closet. No borrowing clothes for me this time. I would be elegant and articulate, and with a little bit of luck, I'd be back home before I needed to rely on either of those qualities.

The front stairs were silent, and I was able to get my coat from the hall closet without incident. I slipped into the living room and sat in Grandma Anderson's fancy wingback chair, listening to make sure Mom hadn't woken up. Nothing. Good. I opened Helen's journal, my knees knocking together as I flipped through to October. There it was. The article was dated October 19, 1929.

HIGHEST COURTS RULE IN FAVOUR
OF ALBERTA WOMEN

"Persons" Includes Members of Both Male and Female Sex — Notable victory for Magistrate Murphy, Mrs. Nellie McClung and Their Associates.

CHAPTER 18

Mistaken Identity

"KAMI?" HELEN PRACTICALLY bumped into me as I crept out of the living room into the front hallway. "Golly, you gave me a scare. How did you get in here? We're locking our doors now, you know, ever since . . ." Helen paused.

"Ever since I came bursting through them uninvited," I finished the sentence for her.

"Well, Dad says Edmonton is growing quickly, so it wouldn't hurt to keep them locked," she added, not wanting to hurt my feelings.

"That's okay. I understand. Hey, you got your hair cut," I said, noticing the sleek bob. "You look older."

Helen beamed at that comment. "I'm thirteen now. Look." She held out her right hand and wiggled her ring finger, showing off a shiny gold ring with a tiny sapphire. "Mom and Dad gave it to me for my birthday."

"It's beautiful. I wish I could have been here for your birthday," I said, staring into the thirteen-year-old face of my great-grandmother. It was impossible to believe and yet, here she was.

"You're looking at me funny," Helen said, scrunching up her face. "Do I have jam on my face?"

"No. I was just wondering if your mother was home."

Helen shook her head. "She's at the newspaper office."

"Good." I felt myself relax a little.

"Oooh. You look fancy," Helen said, when I took off my coat. "Are you here for the party?"

"What party?"

"Mother is having the Canadian Women's Press Club meeting here tonight. They're celebrating the signing of those papers in London. You know, the thing Mrs. Murphy was working on so that women could be people the same as men."

"You're having a celebration for the Women as Persons case here? Tonight?"

"Yes. Mother is positively thrilled about it."

"The Famous Five are coming here?" Wow.

"Yes, and I am going to take coats and maybe even serve tea. I only hope I don't spill tea on the white tablecloth. I'd just die." Helen stopped for breath.

"You won't." I laughed. "I can't believe those famous women are all going to be here. That's just crazy. Do you realize what they accomplished? People will write about it in history books, and talk about it in school forever."

"Stop talking like that. I'm nervous enough as it is."

I followed Helen into the kitchen.

"You get out the silver and shine it up, and I'll fill the sugar bowl."

"Does the silver have to be polished *every* time you use it?" I asked, taking the soft cloth out of the silver chest.

"No, only when we have company."

"Well, I have to say I'm glad Mom doesn't own any real silver. I had no idea that it tarnished so easily."

"I know!" Helen said suddenly. "Why don't I ask Mother if you can serve tea, too? Wouldn't that be fun?"

"Do you think she would let me?" What would my teacher think if she could see me visiting with the Famous Five? Then I remembered my speedy exit from the Murphy house. "Mrs. Murphy might be surprised to see me. I'm not sure she'll want me serving tea at her special celebration."

"Where did you go, anyway?" Helen asked. "Mrs. Murphy told Mom that you snuck out of the house and ran away. There was steam coming out her ears that day and that's not a word of a lie."

"Yeah, I bet. I didn't want to make her mad, but I had to do something. That woman from the Children's Aid came to the house."

"Well, you are a sneaky one, that's for sure and for certain."

"You're the one who told me that they wanted to cart me off to Ponoka," I said, defending myself.

"You've a point there. But where did you go?"

"I ran to the library. There was a newspaper article about the pilots' homecoming, so I started to read it. That's when everything changed again and I was back in my own neighbourhood."

"Gee, Kami. That gives me goose bumps."

"I know. Me too." I paused, wanting to choose the right words. "What would you say if I asked you to do me a favour?"

"Is it dangerous?" Her eyes grew wide.

"No, of course not. And it's nothing that would get you into trouble. It's actually very simple."

"First tell me what it is."

A door slammed in the hall. Oh no.

"Hello, anybody home?" Mrs. Mitchell called from the front hall.

"Now, what?" I mouthed the words to Helen.

"I'll tell mother you were wondering how she was doing after the accident, and that I invited you in," Helen whispered.

Escape routes were limited. Run outside or greet Mrs. Mitchell. Those were the choices. Oh, why hadn't we gone to Helen's bedroom where I could at least hide in the closet? The kitchen door swung open, making my decision for me.

Mrs. Mitchell stared at me, looking confused. "Kami? Is

that you? You look ... different. Does Mrs. Murphy know you are here?"

"No, I came here first. I wanted to visit Helen. And to see how you were doing since the accident," I added at the last minute. "I guess everyone is pretty mad at me."

"I don't know that *everyone* is mad at you. It's a trifle difficult to feel anger toward a person who saves one's life," Mrs. Mitchell said matter-of-factly. "But if I were Mrs. Murphy, I would indeed be disappointed *and* angry."

From the stern look on her face, I knew Mrs. Mitchell had more to say on the matter.

"Mrs. Murphy is a police magistrate, a judge. She is a woman of influence and power. A person to be admired but, more importantly, to be respected. How do you think she felt when you ran off right under her nose, as though she could not control a young girl whom she employed in her own home?"

"It wasn't my intention to embarrass Mrs. Murphy. I was terrified that the Children's Aid lady was going to take me away and send me to some awful place, or have me locked up."

"For heaven's sake, no one is going to lock you up," Mrs. Mitchell said. "Where would you get a ridiculous notion like that?"

"I thought that's what Mrs. Murphy said," I mentioned vaguely.

"I overheard your conversation with Mrs. Murphy, Mother," Helen stated.

Mrs. Mitchell faced her daughter. "First of all, you know better than to eavesdrop on conversations, and secondly, I have no idea what conversation you're talking about."

"You said that Kami might need to go to Ponoka."

Mrs. Mitchell's eyes widened with surprise. "There was no such conversation, Helen. I am shocked you would say such a thing. You told Kami this?"

"Yes, Mother," Helen answered. "But I was worried for Kami. Honestly, I did hear you talk about Ponoka. I didn't mean to cause trouble."

"Ponoka?" Mrs. Mitchell paused in thought and then recognition sparked in her eyes. "For the love of Pete, Helen, you've made a serious error. Kami was not the subject of that particular conversation. We were talking about poor old Mrs. McArthur, next door. She left her home one day without getting dressed, and she knocks on our door at all times of day and night. I was asking for Mrs. Murphy's advice because I haven't been able to get hold of the woman's son."

"But," Helen argued, "you said, you didn't know where her family was, and . . ." Helen paused, the realization of her mistake sinking in. "Oh my gosh, Kami, I'm so sorry. I was sure I heard mother say your name, but now that I think about it, I don't think she did." Colour drained from Helen's face. "This is all my fault."

The clock in the hall chimed five times. "Good heavens. I came home early to prepare for this evening's celebration, and I've not got a blessed thing done. You two girls are going to have to help if we're to do justice to this celebration."

"Here is an apron to cover your dress, Kami." Her eyes narrowed suspiciously. "One might think you had dressed for a party this evening."

"I wore a dress to visit this time, because my other clothes were not very suitable. I had no idea about the celebration."

"At any rate, it would seem that my daughter was responsible for your disappearance. I must admit, given your situation, I would probably have run away as well. Although . . . if you were able to go home in the first place . . ." Mrs. Mitchell shook her head. "There are a lot of unanswered questions but those will have to wait for another time. Right now, we have a party to prepare."

And just like that, I found myself setting out cups and saucers in anticipation of the arrival of the Famous Five.

CHAPTER 19

The Famous Five

HELEN SAT ON THE BED, looking into the mirror above her dresser. She dipped her fingers in a jar of Brilliantine. "This cream makes your hair silky soft and shiny. I borrowed this from Mom, just for tonight." Helen smoothed the cream over her short bob. By the time she finished, there wasn't a hair out of place. "Is it shiny?" she asked, patting her hair again.

"Like glass," I said. "Look, I don't even need a mirror. I can see my reflection in your hair." I bent over her head, pretending to admire myself.

Helen laughed. "You're so funny."

I smoothed a bit of Brilliantine on my fly-away strands. "I

really hope Mrs. Murphy isn't still furious with me. I would give anything to be a mouse in the corner tonight." Mrs. Murphy was to have the final say regarding my serving tea at the celebration.

"Helen, hurry up. The ladies will be here any moment, and you have to be ready to take their coats," Mrs. Mitchell called up the stairs.

"Coming," Helen yelled down, then she turned to me, "I'll come back upstairs and let you know as soon as I find out anything." She smoothed her fingers over her hair one more time before dashing out the door.

Voices of the arriving guests floated up the stairwell, re-minding me of the New Year's Eve party. Even from behind the closed door, I could imagine the excitement building in anticipation of the influential women being honoured to-night.

I found a copy of *The Chatelaine* magazine lying beside Helen's bed. Isn't that funny, I thought, picking it up off the floor, that it used to be called *The Chatelaine*. It also made me wonder who or what a "chatelaine" actually was. Well, what-ever it was, seventy-five years was a pretty good run for a magazine. The pictures advertised new styles with higher hemlines and fancy new electric stoves, but nothing of any particular interest to me.

Oh why hadn't Helen come back yet? Mrs. Murphy must have arrived by now. I stared out the window. Too bad it didn't look onto the driveway where I could watch everyone arrive. I opened the door a crack, trying to hear Mrs. Murphy's voice, but a cacophony of high-pitched voices filled the air.

A few moments later, the chattering voices and laughter subsided, signalling, I supposed, the beginning of the meeting. Mrs. Murphy must have refused to include me tonight. I didn't really blame her, but it was hugely disappointing. Helen was probably too busy with the guests to come back and tell me. I flopped onto Helen's bed, not caring if my hair got messed up. How could I be so close and yet not even be allowed to catch a glimpse of the women? It wasn't fair.

Sounds of applause vibrated through the floor, adding to my frustration on missing out. Hiding out in Helen's room made no sense. Now that I thought about it, no one said anything about not listening to the women. As long as Emily Murphy couldn't see me, what harm would there be in listening? I softly opened the door and crept into the hall. I snuck part way down the stairs where I couldn't be seen.

Emily Murphy was being introduced as the past president and long time member of the Women's Press Club. "We all knew that Emily Murphy would do great things when she was appointed the first police magistrate in the entire British Empire. But I don't know if any of us could have predicted that she would march her cause, our cause, all the way to the Privy Council in London to win this battle for all women."

The New Year's Eve party flashed through my head. Maybe I could watch from behind the coats. None of the women would leave in the middle of the speeches. It wasn't a fool-proof plan, but I was desperate enough to believe it would work.

"I once heard our Emily say that the world loves a peaceful man, but gives way to a strenuous kicker," the speaker continued. "I think you'll agree with me that there is not a more strenuous kicker to be found in Canada than Emily Murphy, but I guess the Supreme Court Justices found that out, didn't they, ladies?" There was a lot of clapping and cheering at this point, giving me the opportunity to make a quick dash into the alcove where the coats were hung. I huddled on the bench, pulling up my legs to hide behind one of the long wool coats. Sitting as still as humanly possible, I strained to hear every word. Thank goodness, the double doors into the living room had been left open.

"Each of these women, highly successful in her own right, will be asked to speak to this astounding achievement and then we will open it up for questions. We will ask the illustrious leader and fearless judge, Emily Murphy, to begin and then to introduce each of her esteemed colleagues."

When Emily Murphy stood to speak, the room fell silent, and every head turned toward her. You could feel the atmosphere of respect as the audience soaked in her every word.

"For twelve years I have tried everything in my power to have women recognized as persons — to have the British North America Act interpreted in a way that includes women. Petition after petition to have a woman appointed to the

Senate was turned away because the Supreme Court of Canada refused to acknowledge that the word *persons* included women. I always said, you can't leave anything to chance; everything has to be pushed from behind." More cheers. "As soon as my brother Bill pointed out that there was a provision in the Supreme Court Act, whereby five people could seek the interpretation of a constitutional point, I knew what needed to be done. I gathered my team of Alberta reformers, and push we did. We pushed this thing clear through to the Lords of the Privy Council, where common sense prevailed. But none of this would have been possible without these women who join me here tonight, and who are every bit as deserving of the glory and the celebration."

Emily Murphy then introduced her friend and eager supporter, Nellie McClung.

"I never despaired of ultimate victory and I am thrilled to have played a part," Mrs. McClung began, "but truly the credit goes to my dear friend and colleague, Emily, who refused to accept the ruling of the Supreme Court of Canada. A lesser *person*," Nellie McClung spoke with deliberate emphasis on the word *person*, "would have admitted defeat at this point. But the determined woman before you this evening denies the very existence of the word *defeat*. It was she who wrote all the letters and arranged every detail in the controversy, assuming all the labour and the expense involved. Her handling of the whole matter has been a masterpiece of diplomacy, and to her the victory belongs." Nellie McClung paused while the audience applauded and I took the opportunity to stretch my leg, tingling from my cramped position. I peeked from behind the coats, but I couldn't see Helen anywhere.

Mrs. Parlby, a petite lady, was introduced as the "Minister of Cooperation," but her voice was quiet and I couldn't follow much of what she was saying. I was going to turn into Gumby if I stayed here any longer. Just when I was about to slip out from behind the coats, a woman turned in her chair and looked right at me, or so it seemed. I pressed myself to the wall and didn't dare peek through the coats for a few minutes. I was about to try again when Mrs. Mitchell announced that it was time for refreshments. Yikes. Now what? Women milled around getting tea and chatting. It looked like I was stuck.

"Millie," a voice called out from the group of ladies, "if you hired a domestic, why do you have your daughter serving the tea this evening? Now, now, you can admit that you broke down and hired a servant girl. We won't hold it against you."

"Really Audrey, I haven't the slightest inclination to hire help. Besides, Helen is only too pleased to join us tonight, aren't you, dear?"

"Mother, may I speak to you a moment?" Helen tried to get her mother's attention, but the Audrey lady wasn't finished yet.

"At any rate, the girl you didn't hire is hiding in the cloak room."

Oh no. Embarrassment pricked my face, turning it to what

was probably a vivid shade of red. To make matters worse, I tripped on a scarf while trying to exit the coats and fell hard with a thud to the floor. Conversation stopped. All I could hear was the pounding of my heart.

As I slowly got to me feet I could feel their eyes upon me. "I wanted to catch a glimpse of the famous women," I said, by way of explanation. It was then that I spotted Emily Murphy, who, to my surprise, was smiling.

"Good heavens, Kami," Mrs. Mitchell's voice was quiet but firm. "I know you wished to be included, but hiding in the coats, honestly." Then she introduced me as a friend of her daughter. The lady named Audrey, with her smug smile, obviously didn't believe her.

"I'm very sorry," I said to Mrs. Mitchell. "It was a bad idea. I'll go up to Helen's room and not even show a fingernail out the door for the rest of the evening."

"First you have some business to attend to, I believe." She gestured toward Emily Murphy, who appeared completely amused by the proceedings.

This was not at all how I pictured my return to 1929. I took a gulp of air and willed my knees to stop knocking, then I held my head high and approached the chair where Emily Murphy was surrounded by a group of ladies, all staring at me.

"Excuse me for a moment, ladies, there is a young woman here I need to speak with."

I tried to smile, but my lips quivered. "Congratulations,

Mrs. Murphy. This is a great achievement."

"Thank you Kami. It is something you predicted, if I remember correctly."

"I'm sorry about running off, after you so thoughtfully took me in. I was frightened of the Children's Aid woman." I paused, trying to breathe. I saw eyebrows rising all around me. Maybe that was the wrong thing to say.

When Mrs. Murphy laughed in response, I began to relax. "A little birdie told me about the misunderstanding." Her eyes narrowed. "Some sort of foolishness about the Ponoka Mental Hospital?"

"It did put a scare into me. Helen really thought you were talking about me."

"I hope you both take that as a lesson as to the rumours that can result from eavesdropping."

I nodded. "I've learned a lot of lessons recently."

Mrs. Mitchell ended the conversation by informing Mrs. Murphy that the meeting was about to resume.

"I'll go upstairs now and keep out of your way," I said, shifting awkwardly from one foot to the other.

"You'll do no such thing," Emily Murphy stated emphatically. "You and Helen will join us. It is for your generation that we fight the good fight." She rose then, and took her place at the front of the room as the ladies filed into the living room and back to their seats.

I couldn't believe my luck as Helen and I were ushered into two seats at the very back of the room. Two women right in front of us turned and scowled, and I heard another woman mutter something about it being a mistake to allow *that girl* to join the celebration. But I looked straight ahead as though I hadn't heard a thing. Then Mrs. McClung spoke again.

"As journalists, writers and activists, each one of us in this room strives daily to be an agent of change. Part of our mandate is to raise the next generation of women to be strong and confident. Women who will take up the torch when we have passed on to the next world. There is never a wrong time to be a positive role model, and I trust we all welcome that opportunity this evening." Nellie McClung sat down, and then Emily Murphy introduced the next speaker.

Louise McKinney began to address the group, but my mind was still on Nellie McClung's comment about being an agent of change. If that was true, why didn't anyone care about the fact that Asian Canadians couldn't vote, as Mom had said? Why was no one interested in changing that? The emcee had mentioned there would be a question period. Well, that's the question I wanted answered.

Henrietta Muir was the final speaker of the night. Like the other speakers, she had an impressive list of accomplishments to her credit. Every one of these women made personal sacrifices, working to improve the lives of women and children.

Finally, the emcee announced that the guests would take a few questions from the floor. I glanced around to see if any of the women had questions. Several eager journalists already waved their hands to ask questions, so I shot my hand in the air as well. To my surprise, Emily Murphy spoke to me.

"Kami, do you have a question for us?"

"Yes, Mrs. Murphy," I said, but as my eyes met hers, I saw not only a famous judge and activist for women's rights, but a woman who had taken me in when no one else would. The words I had planned to say, now stuck in my throat. These were amazing women who had accomplished great things. Who was I to say they hadn't done enough?

"Kami? Did you forget what you were going to ask?"

"I was thinking about how to choose my words," I said, and then I knew the question I wanted to ask. "I was wondering what you would like the history books to say about you in the twenty-first century? How do you want to be remembered by future generations?"

The audience was silent. When Mrs. Murphy didn't answer right away, I wondered if this was a dumb thing to ask.

"I am impressed, Kami," Mrs. Murphy began, her smile warming her face. "That is a better question than many adults ask, and I am happy to answer it."

I breathed a sigh of relief. And then, the leader of the Famous Five looked directly at me as though I were the only person in the room. "It is my goal to leave the world a better place than when I entered it. I view myself as a woman of action. Every day I pray that I may improve the life of someone whose path crosses mine. Perhaps it is less important how the history books remember me than how the people whose lives I touch remember me."

I thought of Ms. Williams' questions for my Social Studies class. Were Emily Murphy and her famous team racist? Should they be considered heroes for what they accomplished? There was no longer any doubt in my mind as to which side of the debate my argument would defend.

∽

"Did you see the looks on their faces when you asked that question?" Helen commented as we washed the evening's dishes. "They thought it would be some silly-girl kind of question. But you showed them."

"I was super nervous."

"You didn't act nervous at all. You sounded extreeeeemely smart."

"Aw thanks, Helen. I didn't feel very smart when I fell out of the cloak room."

Helen laughed. "It was a dramatic entrance, but then I've come to expect that from you, Kami." She set a stack of dessert plates gently into the steaming water. "I wish I was more like you, Kami. You're so bold. You don't let anyone push you around."

"I'm not sure *bold* is always a good thing." I sighed. I was going to miss Helen a lot. I set the last plate on the table for Mrs. Mitchell to put away in her china cabinet. It was time to go. And this time, I was hoping for a less dramatic exit.

"Hey, you haven't told me the reason why you stopped by," Helen said as she gave the table a final wipe. "And what was the favour?"

"Well, I don't know. It was kind of a dumb idea."

"You have to at least tell me about it. I've been thinking about it all night."

"Well . . ." I hesitated.

"C'mon, Kami."

"Okay, but we need your journal. Is it upstairs?"

"Yes, it's in my secret hiding spot. Do you want me to get it?"

"Why don't we just go up to your room?" I didn't want Mrs. Mitchell interrupting us, or snooping to see what we were doing.

"This is so exciting," Helen said as we climbed the stairs to her room. "Everything about you is a mystery." Helen reached to the back of her closet and pulled out her journal. A large piece of newspaper stuck out of it.

"Look at this, Kami," Helen said, pulling it out and unfolding it. "This is the piece Mom wrote."

"That is so cool. Maybe your mother will get more real news articles, now."

"Maybe. The *Edmonton Journal* still printed this in the society section, but it's a start, I guess."

"I want to write something in your journal. But you can't look at it until after I'm gone."

Helen gave me a funny, sad sort of look. "You're an odd

duck, Kami Anderson. Does this mean you're never coming back?"

"Never is a long time. I didn't think I would be back this time."

Helen handed me her journal and a pencil from her desk. I began to write, the pencil quivering in my hand. There was so much that I wanted to say, and yet it was hard to find the right words. Just then, the front door slammed shut, and I heard Mrs. Mitchell treading up the stairs. It was time to go.

I gave Helen a huge hug. "You're my BFF."

"What's that?"

"Best Friend Forever."

"I like that, Kami."

Mrs. Mitchell knocked on the door. "Helen, is Kami in there with you?"

I shook my head and picked up the newspaper clipping.

"No, Mom. She had to go home. I'll talk to you in a minute, I'm just getting on my pyjamas."

I picked up the newspaper clipping and began to read:

HIGHEST COURTS RULE IN
FAVOUR OF ALBERTA WOMEN

"Persons" Includes Members of Both Male and Female Sex — Notable victory for Magistrate Murphy, Mrs. Nellie McClung and Their Associates.

Contrary to the Supreme Court, the Privy Council today came to the conclusion that the word "persons" includes members of both the male and female sex . . .

The pressure tightened on my skull and my eyes blurred. My range of vision grew smaller and smaller, like a dark tunnel closing around me, until everything was black. The last thing I remembered hearing was Mrs. Mitchell's loud sigh outside the door. When the pressure eased, I opened my eyes. Helen was gone.

CHAPTER 20

The Birthday Dinner

"I CAN'T BELIEVE YOU'RE doing homework on your birthday," Drew said.

The debate was in a couple of days, and I was at the library again today, getting prepared. "The closing argument has to be solid. I don't want there to be any holes."

"So . . . any other plans?"

"Nothing much. Mom and I will probably go out for supper. Something like that."

"I guess it's tough not being with your friends for your birthday."

"Yeah, my friend Becca and I were going to have a joint

birthday party. I told her I would fly back for it, but that's not happening."

Drew packed up his computer and put on his coat. "Go home, or go shopping or something," he said. "You're making me depressed. Even I don't do school work on my birthday."

"I know, I know. I'm going, really."

Drew sauntered out of the library, his backpack slung over his shoulder. He looked as if he didn't have a care in the world. The fact that my father had dropped out of my life hit me particularly hard on my birthday. I mean, that's the day your parents are supposed to remember the amazing day when you were born and celebrate how special you are to them. It's hard to feel special when one of those parents acts as if you don't even exist.

I would never say this to Drew, but sometimes I wished my father was dead. You could explain "dead." People understood that. It was terrible even to think that way, but when I was being really honest with myself, that's what I thought.

The stack of books on the table mocked me. Who was I kidding? I had more than enough information for the debate. It was just easier hiding out in the library instead of moping around home, wishing my father would magically appear for my birthday. Maybe Mom was right about the counselling thing.

I gathered my stuff and headed for home. The sky was growing dark already as the days shortened on their way to winter, making for a gloomy walk. Vancouver would not be this chilly. Later, I'd call Becca. She wouldn't mind if I whined to her on my birthday. Although I had to admit, her last email did not sound as though she missed me much. She had tried out for the school drama production, based on some new boy's suggestion as a strategy to get over her shyness. As it turned out, she loves it. She sounded like a totally different person.

Mom was already at home when I walked in the door. "There you are. Goodness. I didn't think you'd be so late getting home."

"I was just doing some homework."

"We have reservations for 6 pm at this little bistro that Bernie recommended. Apparently the food is very good."

"Sounds like a plan," I said, trying to be cheerful.

Mom frowned at my faded jeans and hoodie. "You're changing for dinner, right?"

"Yes, Mom. I'll put on my pretty party dress for the birthday dinner."

"If you wore a dress, I'd probably faint, but a nice pair of pants and a top that doesn't have a hood attached, would be appreciated."

"I'll do my best." You'd think it was *her* birthday dinner. I really missed Becca. It would have been so much fun to have a joint party with all our friends. Becca and I would have gone on a shopping trip prior to the big event and picked out complementary outfits, almost matching, but not quite. As it was, I wasn't feeling much like celebrating. Dress pants. I was probably the only thirteen-year-old who even owned a pair of dress pants.

Looking more partyish then I felt in my glitter tunic top and black jeans, I clumped down the stairs to the foyer. For once, Mom had actually changed out of her black power suit. Wow. She looked amazing in a soft pink sweater I had never seen before.

"You look so grown up suddenly," Mom said. "I'd hardly know it was the same girl who walked in the door half an hour ago."

"Thanks, Mom. You look great too. You should wear pink more often."

"High praise coming from my teen fashionista."

"Are we walking?" I asked, getting my jacket from the hall closet.

"Not tonight. No point in having the wind ruin our hair."

The way Mom was fussing over this mother-daughter birthday dinner, I should have known something was up. At the time I thought she was just trying to make up for the birthday party I wasn't having.

The restaurant was quaint and cozy. We were seated at the best table — right beside the fireplace. A vase overflowing with colourful daisies sat in the middle of the table.

"Go ahead, read the card," Mom said, indicating the little white envelope propped against the vase.

My heartbeat quickened as I opened the tiny envelope. Could it be? I held my breath as I slid out the little card.

Happy Birthday, Kami. Best wishes for a great year. From your friends, Bernie and Drew.

"That was sweet of them," I said, but it was hard to swallow the huge lump of disappointment that was stuck in my throat.

My mother leaned close and whispered, "Pull yourself together. You can't show that face at your birthday dinner. You're a lucky girl to have friends already."

To Mom, it was all about *face*. As long as your face said *everything is wonderful*, that's what mattered.

"I can't believe you're thirteen today. A teenager, already." Mom opened her purse and got out a tiny purple jewellery box with a gold bow on top. "Happy Birthday, my wonderful daughter."

I opened the glossy box. Inside was the cutest pair of heart-shaped opal earrings. "Wow. That's my birthstone, right?" Usually I wasn't a fan of the milky, rainbow coloured stones, but these ones were pinky-coloured hearts set in white gold.

"When I spotted these in the window, I thought they'd be perfect." Mom smiled. "I've never seen heart-shaped opals before."

"Me neither. They're adorable." I took out the plain silver balls I usually wore and put on the opal hearts. These were the first real jewellery I actually owned. "How do they look?" I turned my head from side to side.

Before Mom could answer, Bernie and Drew walked through the door.

"Happy birthday, Kami," Bernie reached out and shook my hand. "Do you mind if we join you?"

"It's a little late for that, Dad," Drew said, grinning. "We've already crashed the party."

"Thanks for the flowers," I said, my happy-face doing its best. Mom meant well. She was just trying to make the day festive for me.

"Beautiful flowers for a beautiful girl," Bernie said, beaming while Drew looked as though he'd like to slide under the table. I'm sure he was thinking they should have given me a book.

Once we got onto the menus, and Bernie clued us in on what to order, everything felt a bit more normal. It wouldn't go down as the best birthday ever, but it wasn't the worst either. And Bernie was right about the food. My seafood pasta was amazing.

As the waiter cleared our plates, my mother started to act a little weird. She looked at her watch a couple of times and started talking too fast, as if she wanted everyone to get to the end of the conversation.

"No dessert today, I guess," she said. "Next year we'll have a spectacular birthday cake at the house. The timing didn't quite work out this time. Our house is in such upheaval still."

Then, as though following my mother's lead, Bernie announced that he had a deadline to meet.

"Yeah, I hate to eat and run, but I have a massive science paper to submit tomorrow," Drew added, reaching for his jacket.

"That's okay," I said. "I don't think I could fit in any dessert. That pasta was delicious and very filling." It was a lie. I'd never had a birthday without a cake of some kind.

Bernie and Drew walked us to our car, and after a couple of awkward goodbyes it was just Mom and me. I was still wallowing in part two of my pity party, when I realized that Mom wasn't driving home. "Where are we going?"

"For dessert, of course. You didn't think I'd skip your favourite course on your birthday, did you?"

"Well, I did say I wasn't hungry," I mumbled, feeling secretly pleased. Now that I thought about it, I hadn't seen much in the way of desserts on that menu at the bistro. We drove down a side street close to the university, and Mom drove into the parking lot of a little place called Luna Blu.

"Apparently, this has the best gelato in Edmonton."

"Have we been here before?" I asked, as we walked inside. "This really looks familiar." There was a huge glass case filled with loads of flavours of homemade gelato and pretty glass-top tables with swirly metal legs.

"I'm surprised you remember it," Mom said, checking her watch again. "We used to come here on Sunday afternoons before we moved. You were pretty little."

"That's the power of gelato, for you," I said, glad that we didn't have to share this part of my birthday with Bernie and Drew.

"Go ahead and choose a table. I'm going to check out the ladies room. You can think about what flavour you want."

I took off my jacket and sat at the table in the corner. The art work on the wall was a pencil sketch of an old-fashioned ice-cream shop. That was it. That was the shop in the photo of Mom and Dad and me. The outside had been remodelled.

"Mind if I join you?" The voice startled me. It was warm and mellow. The kind of voice that could lull a little girl to sleep by simply reading a nursery rhyme.

"Dad?"

CHAPTER 21

Another Botched Birthday

"I CAN'T BELIEVE IT. You're really here." Suddenly I was six years old all over again — wanting to impress my father.

"Happy Birthday, angel. Lucky thirteen, right?" He set his coat on the chair beside me, then bent down and kissed the top of my head, before sitting down.

Why haven't you called me yet? Why haven't you come by the house? Why didn't you answer my emails? Why haven't you phoned? Those and a hundred more questions raced through my mind. In seconds, my emotions bounced all over the place like one of those crazy bouncy balls. I didn't know whether I should be happy or angry. Mostly I was just confused.

"Where do you live now?" I asked, which sounded really lame.

"Not too far from here, actually. Sorry, I wasn't on hand to welcome you to the neighbourhood. Do you remember that Grandpa went to live in PEI with Aunt Linda after Grandma died?"

I nodded.

"A few weeks ago, Aunt Linda was diagnosed with cancer and needed surgery, so I flew to PEI to see her and to help your grandfather find a place. When Linda comes out of the hospital, she won't be able to wait on Grandpa day and night, the way she has been for the past couple of years."

"Is Aunt Linda okay?"

"The surgery went well so she's in good spirits. She's relieved that your grandpa and I found a seniors apartment for him to move into. It has a dining room where he can get meals if he wants, so he's happy as a clam about that."

"That's good, then," I said, feeling weird about this whole conversation. It was as though Dad thought we'd just pick up where we left off — as if he had been gone for a couple of weeks, not a couple of years.

"I'm glad I was able to get here for your birthday. I told your grandpa he better pick a place quick, because I wasn't going to miss my daughter's thirteenth birthday." Dad winked.

"Hello, Michael." My mother appeared back from the bathroom, her fake smile sparkling.

"Keiko." My dad nodded, but the smile didn't quite materialize, and for a very long minute, nobody spoke. Talk about awkward.

"I think I'll check out the gelato flavours," I said, happy to get away from the table.

"Great idea, kiddo. Can't think of the last time I had an ice-cream cone." Dad jumped up from the table to join me.

I glanced back at Mom.

"You two go ahead," she said.

Dad and I stood in front of the glass cases, checking out all the flavours of gelato. "Don't tell me what flavour you're going to choose," he said. "Let me guess."

"Okay, go for it."

"You're ready? That was quick." He paused and rubbed his chin with his fingers as though he were giving it much thought. "I say you're going to choose," he paused dramatically, "milk chocolate orange."

"Hey. How did you guess?"

"I have phenomenal psychic powers." He grinned. "And I took a shot that it was still your favourite."

"You remembered?"

"Of course. Some of my happiest times were in this shop. That's why I wanted to meet you here. For old time's sake."

So it *had* been Dad's idea to come here. For some reason that made me happy. He finally decided on chocolate-peanut butter-fudge, stacked impossibly high in a waffle cone with sprinkles. He looked like a big kid. When we got back to the table, he pulled a small camera out of his pocket. "Would you do the honours?" He handed the camera to Mom. "On the count of three," Dad said, "we'll each take a gigantic lick of our cones and your mother will capture the moment for all time. Ready?" He counted down and Mom snapped the shot on cue.

"Kami finished grade seven with Honours in every subject," Mom said, handing the camera back. "Stellar grades all the way through."

"Oh, Mom." How to kill a birthday celebration.

"That's my girl," Dad said. "Can't say that I'm surprised. How about sports? Are you still into soccer, Kami?"

"Yeah. Well, until we moved. At my old school, I made the senior team. Only a couple of grade eight kids made it."

"Woo-hoo." Dad gave me a high five, almost losing a huge scoop of chocolate in the process. We both laughed and I began to relax.

"You didn't tell me that," Mom accused, her face pinched.

I shrugged. "There wasn't any point."

"We'll have to check out the club soccer. I bet you'd make some overworked coach very happy," Dad said.

"I'd love to continue with soccer," I told him.

We talked soccer for a few minutes. He told us about a pro game he went to when he was in Mexico on assignment, and I told him about the city championship my team had won last year. We were just getting into a good conversation about the future of soccer in Canada, when my mother decided the visit was over.

"Kami has a lot of homework so we need to be heading home," she said, putting on her coat.

I stared at her in disbelief. "I do?" We hadn't even finished our cones yet.

"Kami," Mom's voice was firm, "I have an early morning, and so do you. It's time to go."

"How about if I drive Kami home?" Dad offered. "That way you can get your beauty rest, and Kami and I can catch up. It's been a while, Keiko."

"I'm good with that, Mom. We've barely had a chance to talk about anything." I shot my mother a look. She knew I needed to talk to my dad.

"Tonight is not the time for long, complicated talks," Mom said quietly. "You can do that later." Then she stood, waiting for me to do the same. I looked at my dad, wondering what I should do.

"It is her birthday, Keiko. There are presents to open. Memories to make."

"Michael . . ." my mother began, but my father cut her off.

"Kami's an excellent student. You said so yourself. Staying up a few minutes later on her birthday isn't going to crush her chances of getting into university."

"It's not a big deal if Dad drives me home, right?" I pleaded.

Mom glared at me as though I was a traitor, then she turned to my father. "Have her home in an hour. She has school tomorrow."

To everyone else, she probably appeared perfectly calm as

she walked out the door, but I knew she was seething. I also knew I hadn't heard the end of this particular incident. But I wasn't going to think about that right now.

According to Dad, the cappuccinos at Luna Blu were legendary, and he insisted we indulge. "You can sleep another night. Tonight is for celebrating."

There was no point in telling him that Mom never let me drink caffeinated beverages. I talked a bit about my friends in Vancouver and about my surprise in being offered the house. I was hoping Dad would fill in some of the missing pieces, but he talked mostly about what we used to do before Mom and I moved to Vancouver. I had finally built up the courage to ask the million-dollar question when Dad reached under his coat on the chair and produced a small rectangular box wrapped in orange tissue paper.

"It wouldn't be a birthday without presents," he said, all smiley and happy.

I opened the box and slid out a double picture frame. One side held a photo of a smaller version of me with Dad, licking the same ice-cream cone and grinning like crazy. The other side was empty.

"That's for the picture your Mom took tonight of the two of us," Dad said. He reached over and squeezed my hand. "You and me together. I swear, Kami, I'm never going to let you out of my sight again." Then he reached into his coat pocket and produced another gift. This one turned out to be a small digital camera. "Awesome," I said. "Mom gave me her old camera but it's really crappy."

"I'm glad you like it, angel. I'm hoping we can do some photo adventures together."

"That sounds like fun," I said, but my heart wasn't really in it.

"What's wrong? Aren't you feeling well?" Dad asked.

"Why did you go for so long without talking to me, or emailing?" The words gushed out. "Why did you just disappear off the face of the earth?"

"Are you serious? That's honestly what you think?"

"It's not what I think, Dad. It's what actually happened."

"What does your mother have to say on the subject?" The warmth had drained from his face.

"How could Mom tell me anything? She didn't know where you were anymore than I did."

"Unbelievable," he muttered under his breath. "So you think I just didn't want to see you? Do you really believe that?"

"Are you saying it *wasn't* your fault?"

"You and your mother need to have a talk, Kami."

"Mom wasn't the one missing in action the past two years, Dad. I don't know what you're talking about, but you can't pin this on her."

Dad just shook his head. The way he was acting made me madder than ever.

"You know, I could have accepted an apology for not bothering to include me in your life, but blaming Mom for your screw-ups isn't cool. Mom was there for me, and you weren't." I was sick of his stories. It was time I grew up. "I need to go home."

The ride to the house was painfully quiet. I couldn't wait to get out of the car, and away from my father who had managed to ruin yet another birthday for me. Thanks.

"There are two sides to every story," he said, as he pulled into the driveway. "You might want to consider that."

I got out and slammed the door, not looking back.

Mom sat in the living room, the lights dimmed, sipping tea. I was hoping she had gone to bed.

"I guess you were surprised when your father showed up tonight."

"Yeah, you could say that." I wasn't in the mood to talk.

"You don't sound very happy."

"I'm tired, Mom. That's all. I'm just going to bed."

"Was it very awkward?"

"No. I don't think *awkward* is the word I'd use. But really, I don't want to talk. It has been a long night and we both have to get up early."

"Your father said something, didn't he? I should have known," Mom fumed. "I knew I should have stayed. That's why he wanted to drive you home."

"Why do you get so weird when it has anything to do with Dad? Why do you even care what he said?"

"Oh, Kami. Your father is incredibly dramatic. Always turning a molehill into a mountain."

"What kind of a molehill exactly are you talking about?" A twinge of fear wiggled in the pit of my stomach.

"Tonight was your birthday, and you're acting as if you

just came from getting your tooth pulled. I thought maybe your father said something to upset you."

Mom got up from the couch and I followed her into the kitchen. "Okay, if you really want to know, he made it sound as though you were to blame for why he dropped out of my life. Why does he always blame someone else for his screw-ups? I hate that."

Mom perched on the stool at the breakfast nook and stared into her empty cup. "What, precisely, did your father say?"

"He said we should talk, as though you . . . I don't know. It sounded like you should have told me something or, who knows. He's just doesn't want to answer the tough questions. That's what I think." I expected my mom to jump in here and agree with me, but the room got very quiet. Too quiet. "So . . . do you know what we're supposed to talk about?"

The fact that my mother wasn't making eye contact was beginning to make me nervous.

"Your father wants me to tell you about what happened between us, I suppose."

"What's to tell? Dad said he was going to move to Vancouver and then changed his mind — right? You didn't want to move back to Edmonton, so you and Dad got divorced. I fail to see what that has to do with his pretending he doesn't even have a daughter for two whole years."

"Honestly, Kami, I don't think I can keep my eyes open another minute. We'll talk tomorrow."

"If there's something to talk about, I want to know now. Are you saying there's more to the story than that?"

Mom poured herself another cup of tea. "My parents did not want me to marry your father. I thought he was brilliantly creative. They thought he was lazy — not good enough for me. When I married your father anyway, they disowned me. I was a failure in their eyes. But when you were born, things changed. They wanted us to move to Vancouver so they could be close to you." Mom paused. "When you were five, I got a wonderful job offer in Vancouver. Baachan offered to watch you while I was at work. It was perfect. I wanted their blessing, and I was very unhappy in Edmonton. Your father finally agreed to the move. He would visit whenever he wasn't on assignment. He had a couple of huge contracts that would establish him as a bona fide nature-wilderness photographer. Then he would move to Vancouver or we would all move back to Edmonton." Mom paused and took a sip of her tea.

"Why have I never heard this story before?"

"The separation was supposed to be temporary," Mom continued as though I hadn't spoken. "I kept telling your father to set up a studio in Vancouver. But it didn't happen. *Everything is too costly here*, he would say. Your father didn't want to move to Vancouver. That was his loss. I told him as much, and I filed for divorce." Mom smiled at me. "You were so happy. Look how well you turned out? You needed a stable home. Not bouncing here and there like some kids do when their parents get divorced. It was the right decision."

"What do you mean about bouncing here and there? What decision?"

"It's a complicated story, Kami. And we're both exhausted. We'll talk more tomorrow."

"No. I'm not waiting until tomorrow. You're talking in circles and making me feel like a crazy person. I'm not asking about why you got divorced. Do you know something I don't know about why Dad didn't contact me for two years?"

Silence.

"Mom, I accused Dad of lying, of not owning his screw-ups. If there's something you haven't told me . . ."

She just sat there, like a stone. A cold, hard stone. There were no hugs and no reassuring words. In saying nothing, she had said everything. My gut ached as though I had just been punched. Why would my mother not tell me the truth about what happened? It made no sense to me. But one thing I was pretty sure about. There was another side to the story.

I left my mother staring into her tea cup and went up to my room.

CHAPTER 22

The Debate

PARENTS AND STUDENTS filled the gym. I paced backstage, jittery fingers clutching my notes, wondering if my mother or father was going to show. Mom and I had barely spoken since my birthday. If she didn't come, it would be the first time, ever, that my mother wasn't at an important event of mine. If my father came, that would also be a first. My mother's reaction that horrible birthday night forced me into the realization that I might have misjudged my father. So, when he called, I agreed to get together with him after school. I felt like an idiot after the way I had acted, but it was time to hear his side of the story.

Ms. Williams appeared backstage to get us organized, and

my mind snapped back to the imminent debate. "You will follow me on stage and take your assigned seats, as we practised," she said, her voice bubbly and excited. Six of us had been chosen from the classroom presentations to participate in the public debate. It was a pretty big deal, especially for a new kid.

"After the welcoming comments, I will introduce each of you," Ms. Williams continued. "One last thing before we go out there. Everyone makes mistakes. No matter what happens, I want you to know I'm already proud of you. Now get out there and shine like the sun."

I tried to scan the audience as I followed the other students onto the stage, but the bright lights made it impossible to see past the front row.

Listening to the other students present their arguments was painful. Kyle, the first speaker on my side, stumbled nervously over his words, as I probably would when it was my turn. Emma, the teacher's pet, spoke first for the other side, sounding like a charismatic politician, which was equally difficult to listen to.

There were three more speakers before it was my turn, and I found my mind wandering back to the talk I had with my dad.

"Do you recall the last time we talked?" He had asked after the waitress seated us.

"I do," I answered. How could I forget? That had been the time he bailed on me at the last minute.

"If I had known that would be my last contact with you

for over two years, I'd have said to heck with the contract. Darn crystal ball let me down again."

There it was again — *if* he had known. I took a deep breath and waited for him to continue. I had promised myself that this time I would not judge until I had heard everything he had to say.

"I tried to call you back, Kami. I didn't know your mother was about to change your number to an unlisted one."

"Didn't she give you the new number after we moved into the condo?"

"Nothing. No phone call. No change of address card. Nada."

"You could have phoned my grandparents." I wasn't letting him off the hook that easily. "They had the phone number."

"You would think so, wouldn't you?"

"You called them?"

"They wouldn't talk to me. They refused to give me any information and said not to call again, that you would be in touch with me, if that's what you wanted."

"If that's what I wanted? That doesn't even make sense. Why wouldn't I want that?"

Dad went on to tell me about messages left for Mom at City Hall, and about emails that bounced back. There was even a registered letter that was returned unopened. "It wasn't all your mother's fault," he had said. "I should have camped out on the steps of City Hall until your mother would speak to me. I should have gone to your school to talk to you. I'm so sorry, Kami, that it has taken this long."

And I couldn't believe that I didn't know any of this? Why hadn't I insisted on real answers when Mom gave those vague responses to questions about my dad?

When he drove me home I had told him about the upcoming debate. "Wouldn't miss it for the world," he had said.

I wanted so badly to believe him.

The student before me sat down and I heard Ms. Williams call my name. When I stood to speak, I saw him. Halfway back, right in the middle. His smile stretched across his entire face as he gave me a thumbs up. Everyone else in the room vanished. For the first time, ever, my father was watching me at a school event, and nothing else mattered. I stood tall, as though wearing an invisible crown.

"Emily Murphy was a brilliant woman, a fair judge, a strong leader and a hero." My voice rang clear and true through the auditorium. "She dedicated her life to the protection of women and children, appearing often before the courts, which was highly unusual for a woman in the early part of the twentieth century. Despite facing disdain and ridicule from men, she was appointed the police magistrate for the city of Edmonton in 1916, becoming the first woman magistrate in the British Empire. As police magistrate, she opened her home to young women, helping them find their way, and giving them an opportunity to better themselves.

In 1929, I could have aspired only to be a maid or take in laundry. I would not have been welcome in the neighbourhood school. It's true that Emily Murphy believed the drug problems and crime stemmed from allowing immigrants into the country — as did society in general. And yes, it would have been better had she stood up for all minorities. But that was the Alberta of 1929. Japanese Canadians, for example, did not get the vote for almost another two decades. Does that make Emily Murphy less of a hero? No. It does not. No one is perfect. Everyone is influenced by the society that raised them and the values they were taught. Emily Murphy fought for what she believed was right, and she left Canada a better place than she found it. If she were here today, I believe she would challenge each of us to leave the world better than we found it. What an awesome world we would have if we all followed her lead."

The audience burst into applause as I sat down. And then they were on their feet, still applauding.

My side of the debate won, with Ms. Williams declaring that the Famous Five were, indeed, heroes. She signed me up for the debate team almost the minute I stepped off the stage, and kids from the class were giving me high-fives all around. I was thrilled by all the attention, but I really wanted to get through the crowd to my dad. It was his opinion of my speech that I most valued, and the fact that he had come, well, I still couldn't quite believe it.

"Congratulations, honey. You knocked their socks off," he said, giving me a hug.

"Thanks, Dad. You being here meant a lot to me."

"Listen Kami, I've got to take off, but there's an idea I want to run by you — a project that I'm hoping you'll help me with."

"A project? That sounds interesting."

"I don't have time to get into it right now, but how is Saturday for you?"

"Good. I don't have anything in particular planned."

"Your mother said I could pick up my storage boxes then, and we can continue our talk."

The storage boxes. Yikes. We did have a lot to talk about. "Okay, Saturday, then."

I glanced up at the gym clock and realized that I was going to miss lunch altogether if I didn't make tracks for the cafeteria.

"What would you say to skipping school this afternoon so that you could have lunch with your mother?"

Her voice startled me. "Mom. When did you come? I didn't see you."

"I slipped into the back row, but I heard every word and I couldn't be more proud of you."

"I was hoping you hadn't forgotten."

Our eyes met. "You were right, Kami."

"I spent a lot of time trying to make my argument effective."

"I wasn't talking about the debate."

"Oh."

"I was wrong to keep things from you. And wrong to avoid your questions about your father. My priorities need an overhaul, I'm afraid."

"I have the name of this psychologist you could talk to," I said, attempting a smile.

"First, I think I need to talk to my daughter."

"Don't you have to get back to work?"

"Not today. Today I am hoping to begin a new relationship with my beautiful, brilliant daughter."

As Mom and I walked toward the office to sign me out, I noticed Purple Stripes leaning against the wall, watching me, and I wondered what she was thinking. "You have the coolest hair," I said, as we walked past her. When I glanced back, she was actually smiling.

CHAPTER 23

The Beginning

"HEY KAMI, how's your morning going?"

I swung around to see Drew sauntering toward me, wearing a blue T-shirt and a new pair of jeans. "What are you doing here?"

"Thought I'd join you for lunch in the school café."

"I don't think they'll let you eat in the cafeteria."

"Oh yah? Check this out." He pulled a school ID out of his jeans pocket.

"You registered for school? Really?" We continued down the hall toward the cafeteria.

"When I saw you on the stage for that debate, I realized

that I missed stuff like that. It's hard to debate with yourself, and besides, I always win."

"You were there?"

"I was going to talk to you after, but you were talking to your dad, and then I saw your mom waiting for you. You nailed it, though."

I smiled. "Thanks. Glad you enjoyed my debut. Apparently, I'm officially on the debating team now. So, you're serious about this school thing?"

"Thought I'd give it a shot."

"Cool. What about your online courses?"

"I'll still take a couple of courses online, but school gives me some more options. I can join a sports teams or," he nudged me with his elbow, "the debate team. Stuff like that."

"And here I thought you signed up to protect me from the mean girls."

Purple Stripes appeared at my elbow, as if on cue, as we entered the lunch line-up.

"Kami, are you coming to the Halloween dance after school?"

"Ah, I'm not sure," I answered. The question caught me off guard.

"Everyone's going to be there." She gave Drew an approving scan.

"Oh, well, maybe," I answered.

"Later." She pivoted on her heels, purple and blond stripes swinging out behind her.

"That was weird," I said to Drew after she was out of earshot. "I would have introduced you, but I don't even know her name."

"She didn't look too worried about it." Drew grabbed a tray from the stack. "We should go to the Halloween dance. I have a great costume."

We. I could feel my cheeks turn pink. I focused on today's menu, hoping Drew hadn't noticed. *We* might go to a dance together.

∽

Saturday morning I sat at my "new" antique desk that now occupied the corner where Grandma's sewing machine used to be. Mom and I found it at the antique store on Whyte Avenue. I was actually getting into the whole antique thing. The old stuff had its own unique style. I liked that.

The bag from The Paper Trail sat unopened on my desk. I reached in and took out the fancy new journal book I had bought and traced the gold-embossed butterflies that filled the large heart shape on the front. It was very different from the smooth leather of Helen's journal, but this one suited me. I opened it to the first blank page. What could I write about this week's crazy events? Did I really want to have the whole mess recorded for all time?

"I'm off to the office for a while," Mom called up the attic stairs.

"Okay," I shouted back. I suspected she didn't want to be around when Dad arrived.

I wandered over to the window and watched her drive

away, thinking about our talk after the debate. She admitted to changing all our contact info, making it difficult for my dad to find us. At first I was furious with her. What kind of mother prevents her daughter from seeing her father when that's what she wants most in all the world? But then Mom surprised me big time, by sharing her fears about the whole thing. The mother who sat across from me at the little bistro was not someone I even recognized. She shared her hopes and dreams for me and how she had been scared that my father was going to strip all that away. It shocked me that she actually thought I would pick my fun-loving, no-rules dad over her — but that's what she thought. She talked about how my father had pushed her to let me spend the summer with him in Edmonton. That was the summer before my tenth birthday. That fall, she bought the condo and changed our phone number and email. She was terrified of losing me.

I sat back down at my desk and picked up the purple pen I bought especially for my new journal:

Dear Diary,
I have learned some pretty big lessons lately:
1. You shouldn't jump to conclusions. Things are not
  always what they seem.
2. No one is perfect. Not even the great Emily Murphy
  or the famous Keiko Kishida.

Just then a horn sounded outside in a rhythmic pattern of long honks and short toots. What on earth? It sounded like a code . . . of course. I ran to the window and opened it. Sure enough, Dad's black SUV was in the driveway. He was honking the American Morse code for the word *love*. We used it as our secret code when we pretended we were secret agents. Dad looked up and I waved, then I raced downstairs to let him in.

When I opened the door, Dad was standing there balancing two file boxes.

"What is this stuff?" I said, taking the top box for him.

"Don't panic. I have a feeling that you are going to love this research."

"Really?" We carried the boxes up to the second floor. "Let's set them down here in the new storage room," I said. "Before we do anything else I want you to check out the attic." We climbed up the back stairs. My dad was here, right on time. Just as he had said. I felt happy little butterflies flitting around in my stomach. We had the whole day together.

"This is fantastic." He surveyed the transformed attic room. "I didn't realize you had turned this into a bedroom."

"Not just a bedroom, a luxury loft," I corrected. "That's why I moved all the stuff to the second floor."

"By yourself? That must have taken hours."

"It did. Unfortunately, not all of the boxes cooperated. The final one leaped out of my hands at the last minute and a couple of things were broken. Sorry."

"Darn boxes. Can't trust them to do a simple job like stack up neatly. What's the world coming to?"

We both laughed, then we went back down to the second floor. I hoped that he'd still be laughing when he saw the damage. He surprised me by telling me that the globe stand was broken when he packed it. That was a relief. It looked like an expensive globe. Then I handed him the picture with the broken glass. "This is a cool picture. Hopefully we can get some new glass for it."

"Ha, ha. Very punny of you. Actually it was not *cool*, but downright *cold* — minus 25 Celsius, if I remember correctly.

"At least you weren't in an open cockpit plane," I said.

Dad looked surprised. "Do you know the story of the Mission of Mercy?"

"Well, I know it was super cold," I said, hesitantly, "and that they were in an open-cockpit biplane. There's an article about it in Helen's journal."

"Ah. That explains it." He pulled the broken glass out of the frame. "You're absolutely right about the plane. I was extremely appreciative that Denny opted for a warm, comfortable plane to retrace the route his father and Vic Horner took seventy-five years earlier."

"I bet Denny May had lots of great stories about Captain May."

"Yeah, Denny is quite the storyteller. He loves to tell about when his dad was in the dogfight with the Red Baron in World War I. It was Wop's first time over enemy lines. Can you imagine? He's one lucky son-of-a gun. Do you know that story?"

"The Red Baron was shot down, right?"

"Yeah, by Wop's captain at the time, Captain Brown. The most interesting story, though, was one about the Mission of Mercy flight. Denny told us about a young girl who ran up to the plane just as his dad and Vic were about to take off for Peace River. She gave the pilots two candy bars which she claimed would give them energy. Not only that, but she assured them that the trip would be a success. She spoke of a re-enactment flight in seventy-five years. At first Captain May thought it was childish enthusiasm, but when things got tough, he clung to her words about a re-enactment flight in the future. According to Denny, in later years, when his dad told the story, he said he was convinced she was a guardian angel."

I rubbed my arms, chasing away the shivery goose-bumps that had popped up. "Really? That's so crazy."

"It gets crazier. After the flight, Wop said he searched everywhere for those bars because they actually did give them a much needed shot of energy, but he could never find them. Years later, when Denny and his dad were on their way home from a hike, they stopped at a Starbucks. And, guess what? The bars were there. Denny laughed and told his father Starbucks wasn't around in 1929, but his father stuck to his story. The chewy fruit-and-nut bars at Starbucks were exactly the same ones that gave the pilots the much needed boost on that cold January day in 1929. Isn't that wild?"

"I think it's awesome. There are a lot of things that can't be explained, don't you think?"

"Absolutely." Dad set the picture back on the dresser. "If

that's all the damage, I'd say you did a fine job of relocating my collection. Hopefully I'll do as well when I move it the final leg of its journey."

That's when I remembered that I had stuck the journal under the mattress — out of sight, out of mind — until I could ask my father about it. I reached under the mouldy-smelling mattress and pulled it out. "This was also in the box. I read some of it. I hope that's okay." I watched my father's face for a reaction, wondering if he had read the journal.

"Your great-grandmother's journal! That's where it got to. I'm glad you found it." He paused, reaching into his jacket pocket. "Which reminds me, I have one more birthday present for you."

"Really?"

He placed a tiny, blue velvet box in my hand. "Your great-grandma Anderson insisted you receive this for your thirteenth birthday. I was going to give it to you the other night, but I decided today would be a better time."

"Great-grandma Anderson? I thought her name was Mitchell."

"That was her maiden name. She married your great-grandpa Anderson in 1939 right before World War Two."

When I opened the tiny box, there was a gold ring with a little sapphire set into the band. Helen's ring. A lump swelled in my throat so that I could barely speak. "I can't believe it." I slid the ring onto my pinkie finger where it fit perfectly.

"Before your great-grandma passed away last fall, she gave me this ring to give to you."

I couldn't stop looking at the ring, my mind filling with pictures of the cheery thirteen-year-old. "I wish she were here."

"I'm surprised you remember her," Dad said.

"Did you know Helen was the same age as I am now when she wrote this journal?" I asked.

"It sounds strange to hear you call her *Helen*. You must have really connected with her through that journal." Dad looked thoughtful. "Maybe that's why great-grandma had this idea that I needed to find you for your thirteenth birthday. I didn't have the heart to tell her I didn't even know where you were. But that's actually what gave me the idea to offer you the house. If there was one thing your mother might go for, I thought, it was real estate."

"You got that right," I said.

"Your grandpa was thrilled about the idea of the house going to someone in the family. I lived here to maintain the property because he was in PEI, but I was more than happy to move into a smaller place."

"So you had the lawyer send the letter to Mom's office."

"Bingo," Dad said. "When your mother saw that the return address was from an attorney-at-law, she signed for it. The rest, as they say, is history."

I wiggled my pinkie around, admiring the ring. "I'm never going to take this off."

Dad wrapped me in a big bear hug. "Now, let's see what other goodies your great-grandma saved for you."

"What? There's more?"

Dad gestured to the two boxes. "These are full of memorabilia from her life. She was quite a woman, your great-grandmother, and she wanted you to have everything. She said you would appreciate it more than anyone else. Isn't that funny?"

"I want to read you something." I picked up the journal to see if the note I had written to Helen that night had survived time-travel. Sucking in a big breath I turned to the back. Yes. The message was there — faded now, like the rest of the journal. I read out loud. *No amount of time or space can take away our friendship. I'll never forget you. Love Kami.*

Dad's eyes met mine. "She had a friend named Kami?"

I nodded. It seemed for a moment as if his mind had travelled far away. And then, in an instant, he was back. "I guess that's why great-grandma wanted you to have it. Because of her friend, Kami."

"Yes, I think so," I said, my eyes fogging over with moisture.

Dad and I brought the boxes next door, where there was more room. Then we got to work on the project, which was to organize all of Helen's accomplishments into a special book that we would copy for family members. I doubt that anyone at that celebration of the Famous Five took Emily Murphy's words to heart more than Helen had. "Canada's Florence Nightingale" one newspaper clipping stated. Helen graduated with a Bachelor of Science degree in health care and nursing from the University of Alberta and then went on to get her Masters degree in supervision and teaching from Columbia University.

I dug through the clippings. She had served in Korea and then back in Canada, became the president of the Canadian Nurses Federation, and in 1971 she was appointed an officer of the Order of Canada.

Suddenly, I could hold all the pent-up emotion at bay no longer. I cried and cried and cried. My dad held me, whispering comforting words in my ear as he had done when I was little and scraped my knee. "We'll continue this project another day," he said finally.

We carefully placed our organized stacks into one box and the things we hadn't got to yet in the other, and I put them in the closet of the room that had yet to be recreated into a TV room.

"Before I take some of those storage boxes down to the car, there's one more surprise for the day," Dad announced.

"I don't know if I can take any more surprises."

"Oh, you won't want to miss this one."

I followed Dad downstairs and then to the kitchen, hoping Mom wasn't home from work yet. What on earth was he doing?

"After you, my angel," he said, holding the door open.

"Happy Birthday, Kami!" Voices rang out as I walked into a sea of silver and pink balloons, streamers and confetti. Standing behind a massive cake that looked like an open book was Mom, architect Bernie, and Drew. Dad took the opportunity to burst into a perfectly terrible rendition of "For She's A Jolly Good Fellow," with the others following his lead.

"Is this like that Groundhog Day movie? Every day when I wake up, it will be my birthday again?" Mom actually laughed, and this time her smile sparkled all the way up to her happy eyes.

Dad gave me a kiss on the cheek, and then I introduced him to Drew and to Bernie. For a moment we all just stood there looking at each other, then Dad reached out and shook Bernie's hand and smiled, and I knew it was going to be okay.

"What about the boxes?" I asked. "Drew and I can help you carry them — right Drew?"

"Just point me in the right direction," he said. "I'll give the really heavy ones to Kami. She's the pro when it comes to moving boxes." I just rolled my eyes.

"And miss the cake?" Dad winked. "Not a chance. But I will take a rain check on that offer."

Mom began cutting generous slices of a chocolate-mocha cake, the likes of which had been banned in our house for years. "Thanks, Mom," I whispered as I put slices of cake on plates for Bernie and Dad, who had got into a conversation about the architecture of the house.

"I couldn't let that awful night be your only memory of your becoming-a-teen celebration," she said, looking down at the cake. I set the plates down and gave her a huge hug. She'd just have to get used to these almost-public shows of emotion.

Drew and his extra thick slice of cake joined me in the sun room off the kitchen. "So what's the secret to this whole multiple birthday gig?" he asked, licking icing off his fingers.

"Guilt. Definitely guilt," I said. Then we talked about the kids we had met at the Halloween Dance and about the Camp Everest fundraiser that was coming up. Kids were dyeing their hair pink or shaving their heads to send kids with cancer to camp. The goal was fifty kids.

"Are you in?" Drew asked.

"I might dye my hair pink, but I don't think I'm ready to go bald. How about you?"

"Yup."

"You're going to shave off all those wild curls? Really? I can't picture you bald."

He shrugged. "It's hair. It'll grow."

"Maybe next year," I said. It would be weird talking to Drew without those crazy curls boinging up all over the place, but hair or no hair I was pumped about hanging out with him between classes. It was going to be totally cool.

It was late by the time I helped Mom clean up after everyone left. Climbing the stairs to my loft I felt exhausted, but happier than I had been in a really long time. My diary was still sitting on my desk where I had left it in the morning. I brought it over to the bed and read what I had written. No one was perfect. I got that right. Perfection, I realized, was highly over-rated. I had always thought perfection was the goal. But it wasn't. Making a difference. That's what was important.

Are you in? Drew's words echoed in my head. I had been challenged to do something to improve the lives of others, and already I was planning to give it a pass. *Maybe next year.* Digging into the zippered pocket of my backpack, I pulled out the pledge card for the Camp Everest challenge. I ran my fingers through the long strands of silky black hair with auburn highlights. It's only hair. It'll grow.

I had no idea what my future would hold, but I made a promise to myself right then that I would make a difference in this world. And I would start by shaving my head for cancer.

NOTES

British Privy Council: Prior to 1949, the Supreme Court of Canada was not the *court of last resort* in Canada. Judgments from cases heard prior to 1949 could be appealed to the Privy Council of England, in London, which was the highest court at the time.

Canadian Women's Press Club: Emily Murphy and Nellie McClung were both members, and the Canadian Women's Press Club did have a celebration for the Famous Five. The details of the celebration as it appears in this book are purely fictional.

Chatelaine: In olden days, it was a ring of short chains that the house-wife wore around her waist to hold all the keys to the various rooms in the home. *The Chatelaine* magazine was first published in the same year that Emily Murphy challenged the Supreme Court decision re-garding women as persons. Later "The" was dropped from the name and it became known as *Chatelaine* magazine.

Emily Murphy and Evelyn Murphy: During her years as police magis-trate, Emily Murphy did, on occasion, hire young women that she encountered through the justice system, in order to help them out. One of her daughters, Evelyn, did live with Emily and her husband. I found very little information about Evelyn, so although she existed, I have fabricated her personality for the purposes of the story.

Helen Anderson's (Mitchell) adult accomplishments were based on Helen Griffith Wylie McArthur. McArthur married later in life and did not have children, but she did in fact achieve all of the recognition and awards attributed to Helen Mitchell in the book.

Newspaper clippings: All excerpts of newspaper articles in the book are actual excerpts from the *Edmonton Journal*, 1929.

Prayer of Faith Statue: This sculpture by F. Fleming Baxter made its home in the Strathcona Public Library for several years before mysteriously disappearing. It has never been recovered.

Radio Broadcasts: CJCA was Edmonton's first radio station. It was established in 1922 by the *Edmonton Journal*. The first commercials were broadcast in 1925. Although the actual broadcasts are fictional, all the information regarding the Mercy Flight is historically accurate, based on actual newspaper articles and Sheila Reid's book *Wings of a Hero*.

Stringer: A newspaper reporter. The name is thought to have originated from the practice of measuring the length of a news column with a piece of string to determine how much the reporter should be paid.

Wilfrid "Wop" May: When he was a child, Captain May had a young cousin who could not pronounce "Wilfrid." Instead, she called him "Wop," and the nickname stuck for his entire life.

ABOUT THE AUTHOR

 Lois was born in Montreal, Quebec, grew up mostly in Riverview, New Brunswick, and spent her summers visiting Ontario. She graduated from Acadia University in Nova Scotia and the University of Alberta in Edmonton before moving to Calgary, Alberta, where she enjoyed a long and rewarding teaching career. These richly Canadian experiences sparked her passion for bringing Canada's stories alive for readers. Her first historical novel, *Winds of L'Acadie*, takes readers on a journey to Nova Scotia in 1755 just as the deportation of the Acadians is about to take place. It was shortlisted for the Hackmatack Award in Atlantic Canada and the Golden Eagle Award in Alberta. In addition to reading, writing and blogging, Lois loves visiting schools, conducting workshops and presenting at conferences. She currently lives in Calgary where she enjoys time with her husband, daughter, son and daughter-in-law.

Stop by her website for a visit: www.loisdonovan.com or email iwrite@loisdonovan.com.

MARQUIS

Québec, Canada